CHERRY AMES AT SPENCER

The CHERRY AMES *Stories*

☆   ☆   ☆

The VICKI BARR *Flight Stewardess Series*

"Seize that man, Dr. Laughton," Casey gasped. "He's a thief."

C. Leslie Thomson, St. Andrews

"Stop that man, Dr. Laughton," Cherry gasped. "He's a thief!"

Cherry Ames at Spencer

CHERRY AMES AT SPENCER

By

JULIE TATHAM

~~~~~~

NEW YORK

GROSSET & DUNLAP

Publishers

Contents

Contents

CHERRY AMES AT SPENCER

CHAPTER I

A Good Resolution

CHERRY TOOK A DEEP BREATH AS THE TAXI STARTED UP the hill. Now she and Josie could see Spencer Hospital, a huge cluster of white buildings on top of the hill. Spencer was really a city in itself with its trim yards, broad avenues, landscaped lawns, and well-kept tennis courts. And to Cherry, in her probationer days, it had seemed like a terrifying labyrinth. But now the very sight of it rapidly drawing nearer filled her with the memories of the three thrilling years she had spent there with her friends who had trained and worked with her until graduation.

Cherry closed her dark eyes, remembering that first week when she, an awe-struck "probie," had met the classmates who were to share so many exciting experiences with her. She could see them now in their humble gray probationers' dresses which they, as student nurses, discarded for blue and white striped uniforms, until at last, as graduate nurses, they had earned the right to wear starched white uniforms, white stockings, and broad black velvet bands on the cuff of their caps. They had herded together as probies, and they had kept in touch with one another ever since.

There had been red-haired, full-of-fun, Gwen Jones; earnest, rather rabbity-looking, but really very efficient, Josie Franklin; plump Bertha Larsen; hazel-eyed Vivian Warren; Mai Lee, the lovely Chinese-American girl; and Ann Evans, now Mrs. Jack Powell. Later, as visiting nurses, they had all, except Ann, shared an apartment in New York's Greenwich Village, No. 9, the headquarters of the Spencer Club.

But a month ago Gwen had accepted the position of head nurse on the Medical Ward of the Children's General Hospital, a new wing which had recently been added to the many white buildings on the Spencer Hospital grounds. Gwen had written enthusiastically:

"I *love* it, gang! It's a miniature of any general hospital, except that the oldest patient is twelve. Besides my department there are Contagious, Surgical, Orthopedic, and heaven knows how many other wards—at least a dozen more than there were in Pediatrics when we were in training. And are the beds ever filling up! So fast that the Personnel Department is frantically advertising in the 'Help Wanted' columns every day. We're especially short of help in dietary and maintenance, but not nearly so desperate for cooks and elevator men as we are for nurses. The enormous clinic on the ground floor is jam-packed from eight to four with only two wild-eyed nurses trying to cope with more than a hundred kids. And as for poor me, I've got only some pathetic probies and a couple of senior nurses on my floor—nary an R.N., although I could use at least three graduates."

Gwen had ended her letter with:

"Wish you were here, all of you, and I don't mean maybe!"

And that was why they *were* here, back at Spencer— Josie to help out in the general clinic and Cherry to act as assistant to Dr. Benham, a famous otologist who specialized in the new radon treatment for children with impaired hearing. Cherry had been recommended for this job by Dr. Joe Fortune who lived in her home town, Hilton, Illinois, and who had ushered Cherry and her twin brother, Charlie, into the world.

Dr. Joe had gone through medical school with the Chief of the Pediatric Service, Dr. Van Wyck Laughton, who had given up his private practice to devote all of his time and energies to the new Children's General Hospital.

"Van Laughton," Dr. Joe had told Cherry, "is an internationally known pediatrician, but you'd never know it from his appearance or manner. He's not much taller than my harum-scarum daughter, Midge, and pretends to be as meek as Moses. But don't let him fool you. All of Spencer's children are his babies, and woe betide the nurse or intern who fails to treat each and every patient as though it were a little prince or princess. He interned there and was assistant resident and then head resident of Pediatrics for many years.

"Watch your step, Cherry," Dr. Joe had cautioned her, his lips smiling, but his luminous eyes very sober. "No pranks. Remember, Dr. Benham will be your boss, but Dr. Laughton is the boss of all the bosses. He has the final word in all the appointments and wouldn't hesitate to dismiss you if you let your impulsiveness lead you into a violation of the rules and regulations."

Cherry, remembering Dr. Joe's advice, sighed and said to Josie, "I've made up my mind to be the most dignified, most correct nurse in the whole new wing. I hope no one on the staff remembers the scrapes I got into during training."

Josie giggled. "If you've really reformed, none of the old crowd will recognize you. Remember how you and

Gwen almost got expelled for borrowing the demonstration doll and the time that white rabbit got loose in the Children's Ward?"

"I'll never forget it," Cherry admitted with a rueful chuckle. "And I guess nobody else will. But Gwen says everyone is new on the staff of the Children's Hospital, and that we'll have nothing to do with anyone connected with the other buildings."

Josie's eyes behind her glasses were teasing. "And even if you should run into Dr. Wylie, he won't order you to wipe off the rouge now that you're a full-fledged R.N."

Cherry laughed until her black curls danced. She had amazingly red cheeks and lips which had earned her her nickname. The Head Resident Surgeon in her probie days had mistaken her vivid coloring for rouge and Cherry had had a hard time convincing him that she couldn't wipe it off.

The taxi stopped in front of the stately central building, Spencer Hall, and Cherry said:

"We want to go to the new children's wing. Is there a separate entrance or should we get out here?"

For answer, the driver started off again. "It's got a separate entrance all right, miss, complete with doorman, and it's a good long walk from here, especially when you've got heavy bags to tote. A wonderful thing, that new wing," he went on approvingly. "We've needed a new children's hospital for a long time."

And then Cherry saw it, a beautiful five-story building, dazzling white in the October sunshine. Young patients of all ages were enjoying sun baths on the spacious porches that circled the building on every floor. Cherry guessed that these children were convalescents and noted with approval that their wrappers and blankets were bright and cheerful looking, and that their deck chairs had been painted the gay, gaudy colors that appeal to children. Even the uniform of the tall doorman who hurried down the wide steps to help them out of the cab had been designed to appeal to young people and to give them confidence. It was a handsome navy-blue uniform, elaborately trimmed in gold braid, with big ornamental gold epaulets on each shoulder. And the man who was wearing it was obviously proud of this brand-new uniform and the cap with the shining gold letters "Children's General Hospital."

He came down the steps with a sort of conscious erectness, as though he were trying to live up to his part by imitating the carriage of a military man. He had a pleasant face and a warm, friendly smile.

"Good afternoon, ladies," he greeted them, reaching in for their bags as Cherry paid the cab driver. His eyes rested for a moment on the letters printed on Cherry's suitcase, "C. Ames, R.N.," and his smile widened.

"I guess you're the two new clinic nurses I was told to look out for," he said. "Miss Ames and Miss Franklin, isn't it?"

"That's right," Cherry told him with a grin. "It's nice to be greeted by someone who already knows your name. I'm Cherry Ames and this is Miss Josie Franklin. We can hardly wait to see what the new wing is like inside. It's beautiful from the outside." She nodded toward the neat beds of marigolds, chrysanthemums, and cosmos that bordered the walk leading from the driveway to the front steps. "I didn't expect to find the grounds looking so trim. We heard there's been a terrible shortage of help ever since the hospital opened last month."

"That there has been," the doorman agreed. "But somehow they've managed to keep things running smoothly, inside and out. Now me, I've only been here a week, but I know the layout pretty well. I'm off duty at four, and I'd be pleased to show you young ladies the way to the Chief Nurse's office then. It's over in the main building, Spencer Hall."

Cherry laughed. "That's very nice of you, but we could find our way there blindfolded. You see, Miss Franklin and I trained here at Spencer."

"Is that so?" The doorman chuckled. "Then I guess

you two old-timers know your way around better than I do. Was Miss Reamer the Superintendent of Nurses when you were here?"

"Oh, yes," Cherry told him, remembering the tall, middle-aged woman who had welcomed them as probationers and started them off on their careers. "I'm glad she's still here. She was wonderful to us. So patient and understanding, especially with poor me who was always getting into scrapes."

Josie interrupted sternly. "Stop reminiscing, Ames, or we'll be in another scrape. We've got to find our rooms, report to Miss Reamer, and get unpacked all before second dinner."

Cherry glanced at her wrist watch. "Heavens," she gasped. "It's almost four."

"Well, that's fine," the doorman said cheerfully. "Here comes my relief now, so I'll just leave a little early and carry your bags over to Crowley. As you can see for yourself, we're connected to the Nurses' Residence by a tunnel," he said, leading them into the lobby of the hospital and down a short flight of stairs near the entrance.

"How wonderful," Cherry cried. "Now we won't have to wear rubbers and raincoats in bad weather."

"Especially wonderful for the late Miss Ames," Josie said with a giggle. "Or have you decided to reform in that department too and get up the second your alarm clock goes off?"

They were down in the brightly lighted, clean-smelling, white-walled passageway now, and Cherry laughed. "I've decided to reform in *all* departments," she said. "I'm always full of good resolutions in the fall. The crisp, cold weather after a long, hot summer peps me up."

"Me too," the doorman agreed. "But I can't believe a pretty, healthy-looking lady like you has any bad habits, Miss Ames."

"Oh, but I have," Cherry assured him, her dark eyes twinkling. "And please don't call me Miss Ames. The name's Cherry, you know."

The doorman grinned. "And I can guess why. Never did see such red cheeks in all my life. They're almost the color of my hair," he said, tipping his hat. "I'll give you three guesses. What's my nickname?"

"Red," both Cherry and Josie said together. They promptly hooked fingers and made a silent wish, and then, in order not to break the charm by speaking before they were spoken to, gesticulated at Red to come to their rescue.

The friendly doorman was apparently familiar with this game and immediately obliged by asking them each a question. Cherry replied to hers with:

"Yes, I was born and bred in Illinois. A little town not so very far from here. Where's your home town, Red?"

But he had already started up the steps on the Crowley side of the tunnel. At the top he left them, and tipping his cap in acknowledgment of their thanks hurried away.

"Now, there's a nice man," Cherry said thoughtfully. "Hope the other employees are as co-operative. It makes a lot of difference."

"It certainly does," Josie agreed. "Remember old Lucy and Mom?"

"I'll never forget them," Cherry said. Lucy had been the maid on the old Children's Ward, and Mom, after her discharge as a patient, had been given the job of supervisor of the cleaning staff in Lincoln Hall. "Wonder where they are now," Cherry said, hoping that she would find several familiar faces in the new wing.

In her room on the second floor Cherry shook the wrinkles out of her uniforms and hung them in the closet, wondering: What would her new boss, Dr. Benham, the famous otologist, be like? Who was the Resident at Children's? And how about the mighty Chief of the Pediatric Service, Dr. Van Wyck Laughton?

Cherry repressed a little shiver and repeated out loud the mental wish she had made earlier when she and Josie had hooked fingers down in the tunnel:

"To the spirit of Florence Nightingale, the patron saint of all nurses, please make one Cherry Ames watch her step and obey all the rules and regulations. *For once!*"

Then, sure her wish would come true, she hurried across the hall to knock on Josie's door. She laughed at the chaos Josie had already made of her room.

"Gwen and I'll help you unpack and straighten out your belongings after dinner." she said. "But right now the Superintendent of Nurses awaits us."

A few minutes later the girls were hurrying through the vast rotunda of Spencer Hall. Outside the door of Miss Reamer's office, Josie suddenly grabbed Cherry's hand. "You know what?" she demanded.

"No," Cherry said with a nervous giggle.

Josie's eyes blinked behind her glasses. "Well," she whispered, "I don't know whether it's the old familiar atmosphere or not, but I feel just like a probie again."

It was so exactly the way Cherry herself felt that she could only nod in wordless sympathy. Then the door opened and out popped an awe-struck girl, capless and in probationers' gray. The expression on her face was one of complete bewilderment and Cherry could hardly resist putting her arms around the girl and assuring her that the years of training that lay ahead of her would be some of the most thrilling years in her life.

Cherry resisted the impulse, but the expression on

the humble probie's face broke the spell. Cherry and Josie stared after her retreating figure and then at each other. Cherry was suddenly convulsed with laughter.

"We're way past that stage, Franklin," she finally got out. "We've got nothing to be afraid of except ourselves. And now that I've reformed, I'm not even afraid of me."

Speak for yourself, Ames," Josie said a trifle tartly. "I'm afraid of everything and everybody in that new wing. And to be perfectly honest, I know I'll die of fright if that big boss, Dr. Laughton, even so much as looks at me."

Cherry sobered as she knocked on the Superintendent's door. She wasn't really afraid of Dr. Joe's classmate, or, for that matter, of anybody else. She only hoped that if the Chief of Pediatrics should happen to look at *her*, it would be with eyes of approval.

It was one thing to make a good resolution, and quite another to keep it!

CHAPTER II

Gwen Gossips

CHERRY AND JOSIE FOUND THAT MISS REAMER WAS AS brisk and efficient as they had remembered her. But she greeted them warmly, her keen gray eyes welcoming them back to Spencer.

"Sit down for a minute, won't you?" she said cordially. "This is an occasion, and two of your old friends are going to drop in to wish you luck in your new jobs."

Before Cherry could guess who the two old friends might be, the door opened, and the attractive young woman who had been their instructor in Nursing Arts came in.

"Miss Mac," Cherry cried, jumping to her feet. "I mean, Miss McIntyre," she corrected herself hastily.

The pretty nurse greeted them affectionately, and

13

said with a laugh, "It's grand to see you again, Cherry —I mean, Miss Ames. Every time I instruct a class in the care of Sally Chase I can hardly keep a straight face remembering the time you borrowed our demonstration doll. Sometimes I could swear Sally grins at me, although I know her giddy smile is painted on."

"Speaking of paint," a gruff voice from the corridor broke in, "will you please wipe off that rouge, Miss Ames?"

Cherry whirled around to face Dr. Wylie's steely gaze. She knew she hadn't been back at Spencer long enough to break a rule, but his very presence made her voice quake as she wailed, "I can't wipe it off, Dr. Wylie. You know I can't!"

And then he was laughing and shaking her hand until her arm ached. "Welcome home, Miss Ames and Miss Franklin. Welcome home." He cleared his throat, trying to speak sternly. "You always did disrupt our routine, Miss Ames, but things have come to a pretty pass when I am forced to transfer an employee from Lincoln Hall to the new wing just because you're going to be on duty over there."

"Mom," Cherry guessed. "Oh, Dr. Wylie is Mom— Mrs. Barker, on the Children's staff?"

The famous surgeon nodded. "She begged so hard I had to let her go. Harrumph! Dr. Laughton is welcome

to her. The worst chatterbox in the world, that woman!"
He strode out of the office and across the rotunda.

Cherry burst into laughter. "It was Dr. Wylie," she
reminded Josie, "who got Mom the job as supervisor
of the cleaning staff in Lincoln Hall. He's all bark and
no bite, isn't he?" she asked Miss Reamer.

The chief Nurse agreed. "He's just the opposite to
Dr. Laughton who never barks and rarely bites, but
when he does—! Well, never mind," she interrupted
herself. "I'm sure you'll enjoy working under him, Miss
Ames, and he's counting on you to do wonders in the
clinic, I know, for we had a long talk about your capa-
bilities only yesterday."

"He cornered me this morning," Miss Mac put in.
"Wanted to know all about you as a student nurse, Miss
Ames. I didn't tattle—much!" She hurried away with a
mischievous grin.

Cherry and Josie said good-bye to Miss Reamer, and
left the office with mixed feelings.

"I feel more like a probie than ever," Josie moaned.
"I'm glad Dr. Laughton is counting on *you* to do wonders, not me!"

"I wish he wasn't," Cherry said thoughtfully. "What
I don't know about otology would fill a medical library."

Back at Crowley she helped Josie create some order
out of the chaos she had left in her room.

Then Gwen appeared, her cap slightly askew and her uniform rumpled after a long hard day on Children's Medical.

"I thought that night nurse would never turn up," she said, hugging and kissing them both. She ran tired fingers through her short red hair, grinning. "Actually she relieved me ten minutes early, but that last hour seemed like a year to me. Knowing you were here but not being able to see you was—well, frustrating!"

"We're here all right," Cherry said with a smile. "And we can hardly wait for you to tell us everything we should know."

"A floor plan would come in handy," Josie said. "That new wing is much bigger than I thought."

"It certainly is," Cherry agreed. "I'm sure to get lost unless everyone on the staff is as nice as the doorman."

"Red *is* nice," Gwen said, rubbing her ankles. "We were lucky to get him. He's crazy about kids and they adore him. Of course the Personnel Department tries to hire people who are fond of children, but we've had to take on so many so fast and furiously since we opened, they haven't dared be too particular. And Dr. Laughton hasn't helped any by firing several employees almost as soon as they were hired."

"Oh, oh," Josie moaned. "There's that dreaded name

again. Give us the dope, Gwen, puh-leeze. What em-ployees did he fire and for what?"

Gwen chuckled. "There's only one thing that drives the Chief into a dithering rage. And that is if anyone—and I do mean *anyone* shows favoritism to rich little boys and girls to the neglect of charity patients."

"Well, I can't blame him for that," Cherry said heartily. "It would drive me into a dithering rage too."

Gwen nodded. "His superimpartial attitude keeps everyone on his toes, I can tell you. He's positively uncanny, that man. Pops up in the most unexpected places at the most unexpected times with absolutely no warning."

Gwen straightened her cap at the mirror over Josie's bureau. "But you two don't have a thing to worry about because you love all kids, rich or poor. Now, the doorman we had before Red turned up was something else again. He was there for the purpose of collecting fat tips and for no other purpose. Naturally he didn't last long. And Red is already one of Dr. Laughton's favorite people. And mine too. Why, he's so crazy about kids he spends a lot of his spare time after he's off duty visiting them in the wards. Brings them little gifts, too. He's always rescuing and reviving flowers and potted plants that would have been thrown out."

"He sounds like a darling," Cherry said. "And he looks like a foreign diplomat in that uniform."

"He *is* a diplomat," Gwen told her with a laugh. "The other day the mother of one of our private patients arrived in a cab overflowing with toys. Red dropped a sly hint and two minutes later most of those toys appeared in my ward. Of course," she went on, "we have adequate standard equipment to keep the kids amused. Books, games, puzzles, etc. But they know they can't take them home when they're discharged and it makes a difference."

"How about the clinic?" Cherry wanted to know. "Will Josie and I have standard equipment too?"

"Oh, yes," Gwen assured her. "But downstairs it's more of a liability than an asset. Some of those kids are little vandals without meaning to do anything wrong. They get restless, you know, and tear up and break and lose things. We simply don't have enough nurses yet to keep them all in line."

"Well, Cherry said jokingly, "all that will be changed now that Ames and Franklin have arrived."

Gwen grinned at her puckishly. "Josie will be a big help controlling the General Clinic kids who raise the dickens in the waiting room, but not you, Cherry."

"Why not?" Cherry demanded.

Outside in the corridor they could hear the bustle

of nurses starting out for second dinner and hurried to join them. During the ten-minute walk to the nurses' dining room in Spencer Hall, Gwen explained:

"Your energies are not expendable, Cherry. You've been assigned to special duty with the great Dr. Benham, and are to have nothing to do with anyone except patients in for radon treatment. Between the in-patients and the out-patients you'll have plenty to do, don't worry. As a matter of fact, I have a darling little girl on my own floor who's due for her first treatment tomorrow. You're to come and get her, so we'll have a chance to see each other for a minute then."

"How nice," Cherry cried. "Was the little girl hospitalized because of a sinus condition that's causing her deafness?"

"Oh, no," Gwen said. "She has rheumatic fever. We've given her a month's bed rest and now that she's to be semiambulatory, she had a thorough physical exam yesterday, during which it was discovered that she has probably been handicapped for some time by slightly impaired hearing."

"The poor lamb," Cherry said sympathetically. "Lucky for her that Dr. Benham is here in this clinic. I don't suppose her parents could have afforded to take her to a specialist?"

"Her parents—" Gwen began and then stopped, as

though what she had to say was too heart-rending to utter. "Oh, Cherry, it's such a pathetic case. Be good to my little Dot Jepson tomorrow, won't you?"

"Of course I'll be good to her, Gwen." They were in the large, attractively decorated cafeteria now, and the girls began to stack delicious dishes on their trays. Cherry was starving as usual, but she was also consumed with curiosity about Gwen's young patient. The peach-and-green room hummed with the chatter and laughter of student nurses and graduates. Some of the latter had been in Cherry's class, although not in her section. But their faces were familiar, though she could not remember all of their names.

At the head of the line at the counter were three women Cherry had worked under in her senior year, gray-haired Mrs. Crofts; plump, middle-aged Miss George, and dour-faced Miss Sprague. They did not seem at all terrifying to Cherry now as they turned to smile at her and Josie. It was hard to believe that once Cherry and Gwen had sighed thankfully:

"We're actually out of Sprague's clutches at last!" The head nurse of Obstetrical had been terribly strict with her students, but, Cherry realized, they had learned an amazing amount during the month they had been on her ward. She glanced at Gwen out of the corner of her eye and wondered if Head Nurse Jones was as severe with her students as Crofts, George, and Sprague had been.

Once they were seated at a table she burst out with, "Of course I'll be good to your Dot, Gwen, but why is she such a pathetic case? Rheumatic fever isn't the dread disease it used to be, and her deafness can certainly be arrested and may be completely cured."

"That's right," Josie said. "Give us her history, Gwen."

Gwen stared unseeingly down at her bowl of soup. "It's so tragic I hardly know where to begin. Dot's only seven and her mother died when she was three. Her father took care of her after that with occasional help from a kind neighbor. Then Dot began to require more and more care for frequent colds, which kept her out of school, and loss of appetite. Finally she developed definite symptoms such as arthritis—I'll never forget how swollen that thin little girl's wrists were when they brought her in."

Cherry bit her lip, remembering similar, pathetic cases in her own visiting nurse days. "And I suppose," she said softly, "it never occurred to her father to call in the district nurse who might have guessed in the beginning that Dot had rheumatic fever?"

Gwen nodded sadly. "I feel so sorry for Jep Jepson I can hardly bear it. I don't care if he is a convicted criminal, I know he only broke into that pawnshop for Dot's sake."

"Criminal?" Both Cherry and Josie straightened in their chairs, forgetting that their soup was growing cold. "Is Dot's father in jail?"

"Worse than that," Gwen told them. "He escaped a couple of weeks after he was sent to the state prison for what was actually a very short sentence. Everyone felt sure that with a good behavior record it would have been lessened considerably. The judge, you see, was very lenient. Just before the robbery Dot began to lose her appetite. She wouldn't eat unless Jep fed her, so he gave up a very good position for a night watchman's job. He couldn't bear to leave her all day, and since she generally slept through the night without awakening and was within calling distance anyway of their kindhearted neighbor, Mrs. Herne, that seemed like the best arrangement."

"I can guess the rest," Cherry interrupted with quiet sympathy. "He didn't get a chance to sleep much during the day with a fretful child on his hands, and so finally he fell asleep on duty and was fired."

Josie carefully polished the lenses of her glasses which had become foggy with suppressed tears. "And then," she finished, "broke and out of work, he got so desperate he smashed the glass of a pawnshop window and swiped some of the things on display?"

"That's the way the prosecuting attorney summed up the case," Gwen said. "And there's no doubt that the court agreed with him. And as for counsel for the defense, I think he must have been convinced from the start of his client's guilt. I only read one newspaper account of the trial, but all of the witnesses were unshakable when they testified that they saw Jep hurry away from the scene of the crime at almost the same moment that the cop on the beat discovered the broken show window."

Cherry gulped down her soup hoping it would dissolve the lump in her throat. "I can see now," she said to Gwen, "why the case is so pathetic. Dot can't stay on in your ward forever, and yet where is she going to go when she's discharged?"

Gwen sighed. "We're all at our wit's end. Social Service reports that there's a terrible shortage of foster homes, and even the few foster parents on their waiting list have stated emphatically that they want only babies and certainly not a convalescent child of seven. With her father a fugitive from justice we can't even try to get some family to adopt her legally, and the orphan asylums are so understaffed they couldn't possibly give her the nursing care a rheumatic fever patient needs for eventual recovery."

Cherry's normally healthy appetite deserted her. She had to force down every mouthful of the food she knew she needed to keep up her strength before a hard day in the Children's Clinic. She guessed that Gwen and Josie felt as heartsick as she did, for they too decided against dessert.

As they strolled across the yard back to Crowley, Cherry asked, "What about that nice neighbor woman, Gwen? Couldn't Dot go to her when she's discharged?"

Gwen shook her head. "Mrs. Herne is an angel, Cherry, and has already carried more than her share of the burden, but she and her husband have nine children of their own. She says it would be physically impossible to cram one more cot into their tiny, over-crowded tenement."

"And I suppose," Josie said thoughtfully, "even if there was enough floor space, Mrs. Herne simply wouldn't have time to give Dot the nursing care she needs."

"That's the real problem," Gwen said. "We'd all be glad to contribute and buy Mrs. Herne a double-decker bed, but it isn't as simple as that, although in the end we may have to compromise temporarily with such an arrangement."

"It would certainly be better," Cherry said emphatically," than sending the child to an understaffed institution where she wouldn't get the feeling that she was wanted and loved. That's more important in the treatment of convalescent children than vitamins, isn't it?"

Gwen nodded. "And Mrs. Herne adores Dot. It was she who called in the visiting nurse the morning after Jep was arrested. Dot had a rather severe nosebleed, and Miss Gardner knew that epistaxis is a symptom of rheumatic fever. Combined with her swollen wrists and generally run-down condition, Miss Gardner was pretty sure of her diagnosis. She sent for an ambulance and that's how it happened that Dot became my first new patient. Since then she's become the pet of the wards; an elflike little thing, Cherry, who lives in her imagination. You had better take with a grain of salt half of the fantastic things she says." Gwen chuckled as Cherry and Josie followed her into her room at Crowley. "Sit down and put your feet up. From now on you're going to need all the rest you can snatch around here."

Cherry perched on the window seat with her legs tucked under her. "Tell me more about Dot Jepson," she begged.

Gwen wearily stripped off her uniform and shoes,

discarding them for a gaily flowered housecoat and green flat-heeled sandals. "You'll never have a dull moment with Dot," she told Cherry. "If she doesn't end up a famous author of fairy tales, I'll eat my cap cuff, black velvet band and all. Why, all during the first half of her month's bed rest she kept trying to convince us that she was a mouse. And now, believe it or not, she insists that her father is a frog."

Josie joined in Gwen's hearty laughter, but Cherry stared thoughtfully out of the window where dusk was painting the yard with shadows. "I imagine," she said thoughtfully, "that the poor little thing is living in a fairy-tale world in order to escape from reality. Does she know that her father was sent to prison, Gwen?"

"Oh, no," Gwen cried, horrified. "Mrs Herne told Dot right off that her father had to go out of town on business, and the whole staff has stuck to that story. Even Leonie Laughton."

"Leonie Laughton?" Cherry repeated curiously. "Who's she?"

"She *is* Dr. Laughton's granddaughter," Gwen said. "And she *was* a nurse's aide. But not for long. She counted on the Chief's influence and tried to get by with gross neglect of her patients, arriving late, and often as not, not showing up at all. But she got fooled. She was fired after one week on my floor. I hated to be a tattletale, but I couldn't go on risking my kids' health. Why, even my dopiest little probie, Polly Dayton, is more reliable. And I had to send *her* to Miss Reamer for a little pep talk only this afternoon."

"Oh," Cherry interrupted. "I'll bet that was the sad-looking little hopeful we passed when we went over to report before dinner." She grinned mischievously at Gwen. "Whew! Have you ever changed! Who would have thought my partner in crime during training would turn out to be such a strict head nurse?"

Josie joined in the teasing. "Imagine reporting a poor little probie to the Superintendent of Nurses. Really, Gwen. I'm ashamed of your heartlessness!"

Gwen hastened to defend herself. "I wouldn't have done it if Dr. Lane hadn't ordered me to. I don't know what it is about David Lane that makes Polly go to pieces, but whenever he's on the floor she can't remember even the little she's picked up. Now, Dr. Dodd has exactly the opposite effect on the student nurses. They heave a sigh of relief when they're assigned to him and always manage to come through with flying colors. I guess it's the difference in the two assistant residents' temperaments," Gwen went on. "Alan Dodd is easy-going and kindhearted almost to a fault. He's so sympathetic he can hardly stand the sight of a child in pain."

"He sounds like a perfect pediatrician," Cherry said. "What's the other assistant resident like?"

Gwen's blue eyes twinkled. "Well, they're both very nice looking, if that's what you're interested in finding out, but don't either of you waste time trying to vamp Dr. David Lane. He's Leonie Laughton's property. She set her nurse's aide cap for him in the beginning, and she doesn't intend to give up now that she's fired. There's a little boy in the private pavilion on my floor, a third cousin twice removed of Leonie's, and she visits him every day in the hope of waylaying David on his rounds."

"She sounds like a vulture," Josie said with a giggle. "How does young Dr. Lane like being pursued by a society debutante?"

Gwen thought for a minute before replying. "The answer is yes and no," she said at last. "I don't really believe David likes Leonie personally—nobody in his right mind could, and he's a very bright young medico. But a lot of people think he does like the idea that Leonie is the granddaughter of the man who makes the appointments. Our Resident, you know, is quitting the first of the year to take up private practice. So both Alan Dodd and David Lane are candidates for the job."

Gwen lowered her voice conspiratorially. "This is strictly gossip, girls, but rumor hath that the prized post of Resident of the new Children's General Hospital will be given to the man of Leonie Laughton's choice. She's the Big Chief's only grandchild, you see, and although she was a flop as a nurse's aide, she's still the last of the Laughtons, if you know what I mean."

"I get it," Josie said, frowning. "If David Lane gets this appointment his future in pediatrics is assured. And the appointment depends on whether or not he's Leonie's future husband at the same time."

Cherry's quick temper flamed. "Well, I *don't* get it," she told Gwen, her black eyes blazing. "From what you and Dr. Joe have told me about Dr. Laughton, I am convinced that the appointment will be given out on merit alone. And I, for one, hope that David Lane doesn't get it. I don't think I'm going to like that young man."

"Oh, but you will," Gwen assured her, laughing. "He's tall, blond, and handsome, and furthermore, if the truth be known, the better pediatrician of the two. Alan Dodd's very traits which make him popular with the whole staff are not necessarily traits which make a good Resident of a children's hospital."

Cherry's anger cooled as quickly as it had flared up. "I know what you mean," she said soberly. "Children require the iron-hand-in-the-velvet-glove treatment. A person who is quick in making decisions and firm in carrying them through gives them the sense of security they all need."

Gwen yawned and stretched. "That's the idea, Ames," she said. "And Alan Dodd, for all that he's an excellent physician, is just a little too easygoing, and to my mind, a mite too kindhearted, for an executive position. Furthermore, which is important, David Lane is the better diagnostician of the two. They say he's never been wrong in a diagnosis or a prognosis yet." She yawned again.

Cherry took the hint and slid off the window seat. "I may not like your David Lane," she said decisively, "but I guess I'll get around to respecting his ability. It does seem a shame though that he can't relax and try to get the appointment without playing up to the Chief's granddaughter."

Josie, who had been frankly dozing, scrambled to her feet. "Good night, girls," she said sleepily. "See you in the clinic, Cherry."

Cherry followed her to the door and said to Gwen, "See you on Medical, Jones, and I can hardly wait. Sounds like a fascinating place."

"It is," Gwen said with a sleepy smile. "Never a dull moment, Ames. Never a dull moment."

CHAPTER III

A Torn Letter

CHERRY'S FIRST HOUR AS DR. BENHAM'S ASSISTANT passed so quickly she hardly had time to breathe. And she felt as though she had tried to cram a year of medical school into sixty short minutes. True to her resolutions, she had leaped out of bed when the rising bell clanged and reported for duty promptly at eight.

"Good morning, Miss Ames," the famous otologist had greeted her with a brisk, friendly smile. "First of all, I'll give you a little test to find out how much you know about the treatment of Eustachian tube blockage with radium extract. You know, of course, that a deplorable number of school children are handicapped by partial deafness which is caused by excess lymphoid tissue and throat-cavity conditions?"

Cherry gulped, trying to remember what she had studied about the ear, nose, and throat. "I guess," she stammered, "in ENT language you're saying that children who haven't had infected tonsils and adenoids removed can't hear very well because one or both of the tubes leading from the throat to the middle ear is blocked."

Dr. Benham smiled briefly. "That's more or less right. But don't forget that even after a T & A, the obstructing tissue can grow back again." He picked up a wire applicator and pointed to a tiny cylinder at the end of it. "The radon is in here," he said. "First we spray the child's nose with a mild, local anesthetic. This is not necessary in all cases since the treatment is practically painless. Next, we gently insert the applicator along the floor of the nose until it rests on the tissue near the entrance to the Eustachian tube. We leave it there for a few minutes and then withdraw it. That's all there is to it, Miss Ames, and usually there is a marked improvement in the patient after only three treatments about three weeks apart."

Cherry gasped. "My goodness, it's like magic, isn't it, doctor? And Dr. Joe Fortune told me that thousands of children who would have been totally deaf when they grew up can now be cured."

The otologist nodded. "Irradiation is a preventive

therapy, not a cure for deafness. Our aim is to correct the conditions which cause deafness, and to cure the millions of children who are handicapped by middle-ear hearing defects."

"It's a very worth-while aim," Cherry said soberly. "I'm glad I can do my little bit to help. I'll never forget that scene in *Huckleberry Finn* where the Negro, Jim, told Huck he would never forgive himself for slapping his little girl when she didn't obey him. Jim found out too late that the poor child didn't obey him because she couldn't hear him—she was left deaf after scarlet fever."

"I remember that chapter very well," Dr. Benham said. "And even today, Miss Ames, thousands of children are unfairly accused of listlessness, inattention, disobedience, and even stupidity, when there is nothing wrong with them except that they are suffering from middle-ear defects which can be cured."

Dr. Benham then showed Cherry the audiometer he used to test his young patients' hearing, and let her examine his nasopharyngoscope, a tiny, wandlike flashlight, which, when inserted in the nostril, illuminated the entrances to the Eustachian tubes. Cherry decided to spend a lot of her free time in the ENT section of the Spencer library. She was terrified for fear being Dr. Benham's assistant might mean she would have to handle all those delicate instruments after one short hour of instruction. She was about to blurt out that she couldn't possibly do anything right when the door to the treatment room suddenly opened and in strode a tall, blond young man in a white hospital coat.

"Ah," Dr. Benham greeted him, "here you are, Dr. Lane, right on the dot of nine, prompt as usual. Miss Ames, have you met our assistant resident?"

Cherry nodded and smiled and the handsome young pediatrician smiled back. "It will be a pleasure to have you in our department, Miss Ames," he said pleasantly. "I think you'll find the work interesting."

"It's very interesting," Cherry said with a rueful grin, "but also very technical. It'll be months before I'm expert enough to give a treatment."

"Oh, good heavens, Miss Ames," Dr. Benham interrupted. "We wouldn't think of allowing you to give a treatment. The residents and interns assist me as part of their training. Your job is to keep the charts and records and, what is even more important, keep the patients who are waiting their turns in a cheerful, relaxed mood. It is almost impossible for us to treat a tense child or one who is frightened in anticipation of discomfort."

Cherry let out a long sigh of relief. "Now I can understand why you took the trouble to explain to me how simple, swift, and painless the treatment is, Dr. Benham. So my job is to reassure the patients?"

It was Dr. David Lane who answered with a nod. "Actually, Miss Ames," he told her, "your job is almost as important as ours. Up until now, with no nurse assigned to this department, it has been up to us to reassure the children. We have wasted many precious hours getting some of them into a sufficiently relaxed mood before we could even insert the radon applicator." He glanced approvingly at her toe-to-cap immaculate whiteness, and his blue eyes twinkled. "We're experts at giving the treatment, but I understand you're an expert in the handling of high-spirited youngsters. You came to us highly recommended, Miss Cherry Ames."

Cherry flushed with pleasure and thought: "Now, that was very nice of him. He didn't *have* to go out of his way to pay me a compliment and put me at my ease. Gwen was right. He's not only very good looking, but he's a very pleasant young man." And she couldn't help wondering if the hints Gwen had dropped about his relationship with Leonie Laughton were founded on fact or malicious gossip. He did not look like a man who would play politics in order to get ahead in his profession.

He handed her a chart then and said, "Dorothy Jepson, Miss Ames. Medical, second floor. She's due for her first treatment this morning. If you'll go up and bring her down, we'll go ahead with the kids who are waiting outside now. They're all old-timers and think of the whole thing as a good chance to catch up on the comic books we let them read during their treatments."

Cherry laughed and hurried out to the big waiting room which had been empty when she passed through it earlier. Now it was overflowing with children of all ages. Some of them had been brought to the clinic by members of their families, but a great many of those in the ten-to-twelve group had apparently come alone.

Josie was frantically trying to keep two of these older boys from putting on an exhibition wrestling match.

"They're bursting with energy," she gasped to Cherry. "I envy the nurse who handles the after-school group. They must be a little more worn out by then."

"They don't look very sick," Cherry admitted.

"They're not any more," Josie told her. "They're all recently discharged patients back for periodic checkups. Poor me, I *would* get a healthy gang like that my first day."

Cherry hurried on and rode up the elevator to the second floor. Gwen, looking very much like an efficient but harried head nurse, was seated at her desk just inside the entrance to the Medical Ward.

Cherry thought she had never seen a place more ideally planned for the rapid recuperation of sick children than this huge sunny room with its tall windows and wide French doors leading to the sun porch. The beds fanned away from Gwen's desk in a semicircle, and each patient was separated from his neighbors by a glass wall.

"This way," Gwen explained proudly, "they can see each other and everything that goes on, but in case one of them should develop a contagious disease it isn't likely to spread throughout the ward."

"In other words," Cherry said approvingly, "they can do everything but cough and sneeze in each other's faces."

"That's right." Gwen chuckled. "And if I do say so myself, the kids have a wonderful time. They often cry when they're discharged, and their mothers write me that they're homesick for us for several days after they leave."

Cherry smiled affectionately down at Gwen. "I can understand that, Jones. Nobody would want to leave a foster mother like you."

Gwen, embarrassed, bent over Dorothy Jepson's chart and began to fill in the blank spaces. "It's not me, Cherry," she said quietly, "although as the daughter of an industrial M.D. in a coal-mining town, I should know how to get on with all types of people. And, when you get right down to it, all people, when they're sick, become children."

"They certainly do," Cherry agreed. "But if you're not the answer, Gwen, what is the secret of the success of your ward?"

"Of the whole hospital, you mean," Gwen said. "Haven't you noticed that it doesn't even *smell* like a hospital?"

Cherry wrinkled up her pretty nose and sniffed. "Um. I've been too busy to take a whiff until now. But you're right, Jones, no antiseptics and no anesthetics on the air. It reminds me of—of, a family wash that's just been whipped dry by a sunny breeze."

"Exactly." Gwen stood up. "And what you can't smell, but which pervades the whole hospital, is the spirit of Van Laughton. The kids call him Van, you know, so the staff does too—behind his back."

Cherry stared thoughtfully at the beautiful fairy-tale murals, the gay blankets on the sturdy maple "youths" beds, the huge doorless cupboard overflowing with toys and games, and the informal shelves of bright-jacketed books.

"It's more like a playroom than a ward," she said slowly. "And the whole building is Dr. Laughton's dream come true. Dr. Joe told me that even in his intern days Van Laughton was dreaming about a hospital especially run for underprivileged kids from six through twelve."

"That's right," Gwen said. "The private and semi-private pavilions are nice, but every time a special wheels a rich little kid in here for a visit, the patient inevitably screams to be allowed to stay." She started across the room toward the French doors. "Dot's all ready and waiting for you in her wheel chair out on the sun porch, talking her head off as usual."

Cherry smiled. "What's on her mind today?"

Gwen chuckled. "We-ell, she's been looking at that mural over there on the wall. The glamorous prince after his transformation from a frog. She says her daddy looks just like that."

Cherry moved closer to the painting of a gorgeously robed young man whose recent transformation was hinted at by the gilt frogs embroidered on his tunic. "There's nothing distinctive about his face," she admitted. "but maybe her father *is* as handsome as a prince."

"Maybe." Gwen shrugged. "But I doubt it. Dot's adorable but as homely as a mud fence. You know the type, Cherry, tiny features, tiny bones, dusty brown hair and eyes, and skin that's neither blond nor brunette."

Something in Gwen's description of the little girl clicked with something else she had told Cherry about Dot, but Cherry couldn't remember what it was. She said stubbornly, "Dot might have taken after her mother, Gwen. What *did* her father look like anyway? His description must have been broadcast after his escape from prison."

"It was," Gwen said ruefully, "but to tell you the truth I didn't listen. He certainly wouldn't return to the scene of the crime, even though the detective novels say they all do. Oh, Cherry," she blurted suddenly, "I wish he hadn't run away! If for no other reason than that he used to write Dot twice a week regularly. She just lived from letter to letter and on days when she didn't get any she would reseal the flap on an old envelope and pretend that it had just arrived that morning."

Tears of sympathy welled up in Cherry's black eyes. "Oh, Gwen! And now of course he doesn't dare write." She grabbed Gwen's arm so tightly that the starched sleeve crackled. "Gwen, I've got a wonderful idea. I'll write to her in her father's place. Couldn't you borrow some of Dot's letters long enough for me to copy his style and handwriting?"

Gwen's blue eyes twinkled. "Not a chance, you lady forger, you! Dot won't let anybody touch those letters except Mrs. Herne. We've all offered to read them to her a dozen times, but the answer is always a prim little, 'Not right now, thank you.' "

Cherry stared at Gwen in amazement. "Why, that's

hard to believe, since it says on her chart she was rather backward in school, due to her frequent absences plus her slightly impaired hearing. So she probably can't read very well, and yet you stand there and tell me she waits until one of Mrs. Herne's rare visits to have the letters read to her?"

"It's a mystery all right," Gwen said with a chuckle, "and one that I'll bet even a famous amateur detective like you will never solve."

Cherry tossed her black curls. "I've already solved it, Head Nurse. Dot's probably backward in some things but very advanced in reading. Any child who has had to spend a lot of time in bed is, and it's the eyes, not the ears, that count."

"Okay, okay," Gwen said, teasing. "But what do you deduce is the reason why Mrs. Herne and nobody else is allowed to read them? Dot is very fond of me, I know, and it sort of hurts my feelings—her attitude about those precious letters."

"That's the answer, of course," Cherry said rather smugly. "Somehow, in the very beginning, Gwen, you must have unknowingly done something that hurt Dot's feelings. And whatever you said or did was connected in her mind with her father or his letters, or maybe both."

Gwen flushed. "You know, Cherry, I think you've got something there. We were terribly busy the morning she was brought in. It was my first day on the ward, and everything seemed to go wrong. Leonie Laughton's behavior didn't help any either. I was so distracted I didn't listen to a word Dot said. She had a couple of degrees of fever and kept rambling on and on until she finally fell asleep."

Cherry patted Gwen's hand. "Well, don't feel too badly about it, honey. She's obviously forgiven you."

"But," Gwen said ruefully, "like an elephant, she hasn't forgotten. Maybe she was trying to tell me she *is* an elephant; she's always pretending to be an animal of some sort. Oh, here she comes with Polly, my probie. Now, I ask you, Cherry Ames, if that kid tried to tell you she was an elephant or a grizzly bear, would *you* pay any attention?"

Polly Dayton was wheeling a tiny girl in through the French doors. Cherry thought with a surge of pity that she had never seen such a frail, pale, undersized seven-year-old as Dorothy Jepson. She was down on her knees beside the low wheel chair in a minute, crying:

"Why, you darling little mouse! I'm so glad you're going to be my patient this morning."

The child's huge gray eyes lighted up and she crowed with delight. "'You know who I am and I know who you are! You're Cherry Ames. I can tell 'cause Gwen told me you had cheeks like two red apples."

Gwen said with a grin, "Well, I guess you two need no further introduction. Better scram, Cherry. 'Bye, Dot. Don't stay away too long."

Cherry wheeled the child out of the ward and down the corridor to the elevator. Dot rang the bell herself. "I can walk to the bathroom now," she told Cherry proudly, "and give myself a bath. I don't like to, of course, because I don't like to get my fur wet. But I'd do most anything for Gwen. She's *nice*."

"She *is* nice," Cherry said, wondering what animal Dot was pretending to be now. Certainly not a frog-child, she decided, if she didn't like water.

Dot chattered merrily on as they went down in the elevator, and Cherry listened attentively, hoping for a clue. But nothing Dorothy said made much sense so finally Cherry interrupted with:

"Let's play a guessing game. I have to find out who you are in twenty questions."

The child threw back her head to stare up at Cherry in amazement. "But you *know* who I am. And I can guess who told you. The Frog Prince!"

Cherry blinked, thinking: "Gwen certainly didn't exaggerate when she said this patient lives in her imagination."

The clinic waiting room was more crowded now, and it took Cherry several minutes to find an empty seat on an aisle so she could sit beside Dot's wheel chair. On the other side of Cherry was a tall, thin boy of about eleven and an elderly little man who she guessed must be his grandfather.

Cherry smiled at the boy and said good morning, but instead of replying, he promptly got up and rudely climbed over her to go to the drinking fountain. Cherry grinned across the seat he had vacated at the old gentleman in the pale-gray suit. "I know just how he feels," she said cheerfully. "It's hard to be pleasant when you're hungry or thirsty, isn't it?"

Bright old eyes twinkled at her from behind huge horn-rimmed glasses. He nodded and returned to his newspaper. Dorothy's voice was now high-pitched with impatience:

"Pay attention to me, Cherry Ames," she shrilled. "Gwen said you'd tell me what they're going to do to me in that room over there." She pointed and read out loud the big letters over the ENT clinic. "Ent," she announced. "That's what you put after a word when you mean no. Like did-ent, could-ent, would-ent."

"That's right," Cherry said with a laugh. "But it's also the initials for Ear, Nose, and Throat, just as D. J. are your initials, Dorothy Jepson." She went on to explain to the child how simple and quick and painless the radon treatment was. While Cherry talked, the blond boy roughly climbed over her on his way back to his seat, and then after a restless minute, pushed past her for another trip to the drinking fountain. When he came back, Cherry said:

"I'll bet you had ham for breakfast. That always makes me thirsty."

The boy glared at her for a moment and said surlily, "I didn't have *any* breakfast."

"That's too bad," Cherry said quietly. "My name is Cherry. What's yours?"

He let out a long sigh of exasperation. "Don't they ever do anything around here but ask you your name?" He thrust an admittance card under her nose. "Here, read it yourself. Every other nurse in this joint has had a look at it."

Cherry saw that his name was Rudie Fowler, but he yanked it away before she could read anything else on the card. Dorothy interrupted then with a request that surprised Cherry so much that she momentarily dismissed the boy from her mind.

Dot, probably in jealous imitation of Rudie, Cherry guessed, was also thrusting something under Cherry's nose. "Here, read it to me," she commanded. "It's a letter from my father. My *fav*-rit letter."

Cherry jumped. This was probably the most flattering order she had ever received in her entire nursing career. And when she unfolded the cheap piece of paper and read the salutation, "Dear Mouse," she understood. When Cherry had greeted Dot upstairs in the ward, she had accidentally called the child by her father's pet name—not quite accidentally, because the little gray-brown mite *did* look very much like a mouse. No wonder the orphaned-overnight child had been hurt when nobody paid any attention to her pleas that she was a mouse, not a dot.

Cherry ached all over with sympathy. The motherless little girl had obviously worshiped her father, and suddenly he had gone away and left her sick and alone to be brought in an ambulance to this big, strange place. If only someone had called her by her pet name it might have made things so much easier!

When Cherry finished reading the carefully printed words in Jep Jepson's letter to his daughter, her eyes were blurred with tears. It had been written by an uneducated man, but by a father who thoroughly understood his child and knew how to appeal to her imagination and at the same time soothe away her worries. Certain phrases seemed to Cherry to stand out as though they were illuminated:

"You'll get well soon, Mouse, and then it'll be like old times. You and me will go the zoo and you can have as many rides on that pony as you want.

"Mrs. Herne wrote me that you go to sleep every night with a great big bear. That's good. A bear is the best animal for a mouse to sleep with now that winter's coming on."

Cherry blinked back her tears. "Mouse," she said softly. "It's a lovely nickname. Would you like me to call you Mouse, Dorothy?"

Dot shook her head emphatically. "Not right now, thank you. When my daddy was away I wanted *everybody* to call me Mouse. But he's back now, so I don't want anybody 'cept him to call me that. Not even you, Cherry."

And then it happened. Just as Cherry was about to tuck Dot's letter back in her bathrobe pocket, Rudie Fowler snatched it away and tore it into four pieces which he flung on the floor beneath his feet. And at almost the same moment, Dr. David Lane appeared at the entrance to ENT and beckoned to Cherry.

A fine beginning for Cherry's first day as the great Dr. Benham's assistant! Dorothy would undoubtedly burst into justifiable tears and remain upset for so long that she couldn't possibly be given a treatment that day!

~~~~~~~~~~~~~~~~~~~~~~~~~~~~~~~~~~~~~~

CHAPTER IV

Putting Two and Two Together

FOR A MOMENT CHERRY SAT THERE BETWEEN THE TWO children, too stunned to move a muscle. And then she heard herself say in a soothing voice to Dorothy, "Never mind, darling, I can mend it with Scotch tape so it'll be as good as new."

Hastily she reached under Rudie's feet and scooped up the scraps of the little girl's precious letter. Out of the corner of her right eye, she saw that the thin, blond boy was crouching away from her with both hands over his ears as though he expected a blow and a loud-voiced scolding. Out of her left eye she saw to her amazement that Dorothy was standing bolt upright on the seat of her wheel chair. She was waving to Dr. Lane, who was waving back just as enthusiastically.

"Come get me, Dave," she shouted at the top of her lungs. I want YOU to come and get me!"

Cherry's cheeks flamed with embarrassment as the tall young pediatrician with a shrug of his broad shoulders strode toward her. Things were getting worse and worse. She was supposed to keep her patient in a quiet, receptive mood, and here was Dorothy dancing up and down like a jack-in-the-box. Furthermore, Dot obviously hadn't noticed Rudie's brutal destruction of her letter. If she had, Cherry felt sure, the little girl would certainly be shaking with tears instead of laughter.

Cherry quickly tucked the scraps into her uniform pocket, inwardly praying: "If only I can calm her down and somehow get her through her treatment before she realizes her loss."

Gently she lifted and pushed the giggling child into a sitting position just as David Lane arrived on the other side of the wheel chair.

"Hi, Dot," he said to the little girl. "What cooks?"

It was evidently a secret password between them for Dot promptly clapped her hands and said, "Pease porridge *hot*, of course, cause the sun's out!" She held up her pathetically thin arms and in another moment they were clinging tightly to Dr. Lane's neck. "This is Cherry Ames," she said, pointing. "She knows my father *very* well. He told her about me being a mouse and all. And *she* told me about how you're going to spray something in my face so it won't hurt when you poke a teeny-weeny wire in my nose, and then when an alarm clock goes off I'm all froo and she brings me back to Gwen."

Over Dot's head, David Lane's lips said: "Well done, Miss Ames." Aloud he said, "Do you want Cherry to come in with you, Dot?"

She laid her cheek against his before replying, "Not right now, Dave, thank you. If she comes in with me I'll just have to talk to her. And anyway, she'd better stay out here and keep Temp company."

"That's right," Dr. Lane agreed, and explained to Cherry very seriously as he patted the back of the wheel chair, "Dot named him Temp, you see, because he's only temporary. In another week or so Dot's going to be well enough to walk all over the place."

And then he and the little girl were gone, leaving Cherry feeling as though she were the most useless person in the whole hospital. And yet there was every indication in the young doctor's manner that he had thoroughly approved of the way Cherry had prepared her patient for her first radon treatment. Maybe, she decided, smiling at "Temp," she was more valuable outside the treatment room in this particular case. Or perhaps the considerate young doctor was trying to make everything as easy as possible for her on this, her first day.

A sharp blow on her white-clad leg brought Cherry out of her thoughts. It was Rudie, scrambling over her again. This time Cherry stopped him with a firm but gentle hand on his thin wrist. The flesh, drawn tightly over the protruding wristbone, felt abnormally dry to Cherry, and she realized at once that the boy was really dehydrated, and that his frequent trips to the drinking fountain were not based on bored restlessness alone.

"I won't keep you a minute, Rudie," she said in a friendly voice. "I just want to know why you tore up the little girl's letter. I can understand why you took it away from me. It was such a very nice letter, and I'm sure you're such a big boy you wanted to read it to yourself. But why did you tear it up?"

He tugged away from her and Cherry was surprised to find so much strength in such an emaciated body. Not too long ago he must have been a sturdy, husky lad. He stuck out a coated tongue at her and growled:

"You let me go. You'd *better* let me go!"

"Of course I'll let you go," Cherry said. "But when you come back will you answer my question?" She inclined her head toward the little old gentleman who seemed to be absorbed by his newspaper. "I'm sure your grandfather will be very proud of you if you do."

Rudie threw back his blond head, howling with derisive laughter. "Ain't got no grandfather. And if I did

I'd hate him. I hate my father, but I hate my mother worse. That's why I tear up her letters just as soon as they're stuck in our box. I hate all fathers and mothers and that's why I tore up that dumb girl's letter." He broke away then, suspiciously close to tears, Cherry thought, and, zigzagging through the aisles, disappeared in the boy's washroom.

She turned to the little old gentleman who was folding his newspaper now, wondering who he could be since he didn't seem to belong to any other child in the waiting room. "He's a sick boy," she said. "In more ways than one. I believe I'll drop a hint to Social Service that his home life should be investigated. He has obviously been treated badly by both his parents." She smiled. "I hope you're not angry because I thought you were the unhappy child's grandfather?"

"Not at all, not at all." He took off his huge horn-rimmed glasses and Cherry saw at once that his twinkling eyes were bright and younger than she had thought they were at first. "As a matter of fact, you were perfectly right. I *am* his grandfather."

Cherry gasped. "You are? Oh, my goodness, now you certainly must be angry. I had no business saying his home life should be investigated without first checking his chart and history. It just seemed to me—"

He interrupted mildly, "You have nothing to apologize for, my dear, and I admire your zeal almost as much as I admire your calm understanding and your patient handling of both of my grandchildren."

Cherry felt as though her mind were reeling. None of it made any sense. Dorothy Jepson couldn't possibly be this kind old man's granddaughter, because Dot had no relatives except her escaped convict father.

"Good heavens," Cherry thought wildly, *"this nice little man is in the wrong clinic. He belongs to Psychiatry over in the main building!* What did one do in a predicament like this? Humor him," she decided, "do anything except cause an uproar in this already too-noisy clinic. *But get him out of here somehow!"*

She smiled at him, hoping she didn't look as tense as she felt. "Do you often bring your grandchildren to this clinic?" she asked.

"Well, yes and no," he said briskly. "I don't actually *bring* any of them here, but I *send* hundreds of them here every day."

Cherry groaned inwardly. "He's downright dangerous. Why, he might walk out of here with any child that strikes his fancy and neither of them might ever be seen again. I've *got* to get him back to Psychiatry. Who is the biggest and nearest person? Why, Red, the doorman, of course. And such an innately kind person, he'll know just how to handle this demented little man!"

Cherry half rose from her seat. "Wouldn't you like to go outside for a breath of air?" she asked nervously. "It's frightfully stuffy in here, isn't it?"

He shook his head placidly. "Why, no, I find it quite comfortable. The air conditioning seems to be working extremely well for once. I told the chief engineer only yesterday that this room must be kept at an even temperature. I'm not going to have my children catching colds in the very place where they've been sent to grow strong and healthy."

He reached out a small immaculate hand and patted her arm. "Relax, my dear. You're just flustered because this is your first day here. But you have nothing to worry about, Cherry Ames. You belong here with us, and I shall always be grateful to Joe Fortune for sending you to us."

Cherry went hot and cold with chilling, burning, dry-ice embarrassment. How could she ever have been so stupid as to mistake the great Dr. Van Wyck Laughton, Chief of the Pediatric Service, for an escaped lunatic? She gaped at him, speechless, as he went calmly on:

"Now take my little Dot Jepson. A child who has every reason to be tense and apprehensive. And yet, due to the way you handled her, she went off for her treatment as happy as though she were going to a picnic."

Cherry found her voice then. "I'm afraid, sir," she

said, "that Dr. Lane had more to do with that than I did."

The famous pediatrician thought that over for a minute. "Yes, Davie Lane is a nice boy and he certainly has a way with children. There's no denying that he has all the makings of a good pediatrician." He leaned forward, lowering his voice to a whisper. "That's the trouble. They're both good men, Davie and Al, and it's up to me to decide which one is the better of the two. They're candidates for the Residency, you know, and I'm the one who makes the appointment." He sighed. "I don't like it. I don't like it at all."

"It'll be a difficult decision to make," Cherry said sympathetically. "I've already heard that they're both excellent doctors."

"Have you heard anything else?" he demanded suddenly. "Any rumors that Davie is a backslapper, a politician? The interns seem to think he'd do almost anything to achieve success. Can't have a man like that sticking his thumb into this nice rich pudding and pulling out the plum of the Residency."

Cherry, remembering the gossip Gwen had repeated the night before, was silent.

The Chief's voice nudged her. "You don't have to be a tattletale, girl," he said tartly. "But after you've been here a while I'd like to hear what you think of those two young men. Joe Fortune told me you were an excellent judge of character. Dr. Wylie, Miss Reamer, and Miss McIntyre all seem to think you've got a good head on your shoulders." He slid off his chair, and Cherry jumped to her feet, relieved that so far the Chief had only received good reports of her conduct.

"Now see here, Cherry," he admonished her. "I don't want you to bury yourself alive in this clinic. When you're off duty, will you go visiting a bit? I'd like you to get acquainted with everyone and everything connected with my Children's Hospital."

Cherry opened her mouth to say, "Yes, sir. Thank you, sir," but he had already slipped away and was mingling with the group of older boys Josie was still having trouble with. And then Cherry saw Dr. Lane coming out of the treatment room with Dorothy in his arms. She hastened to meet them halfway with the wheel chair.

Dot was babbling happily: "—and then, Dave, when I opened my eyes early this morning, there he was, with the most beautiful paper-doll book you ever saw."

David Lane said very seriously as he lowered Dot into the chair, "I suppose you've heard about the Frog Prince, Miss Ames?"

"Oh, yes," Cherry said. "There's a beautiful picture of him on the wall in the ward." She tucked the blanket around Dot's thin legs. "Are there any other in-patients I should bring down for treatments, Dr. Lane?"

He shook his head and pointed to a bench near the ENT entrance. "Those four children are the only ones we can take care of this morning. The big boy is next and this is his last treatment, so you don't have to worry about him." He smiled at her. "If you can condition the others as well as you conditioned Dot, we'll know you've more than lived up to your reputation."

"He's just about the nicest doctor I ever worked with," Cherry decided. "And easily the best looking. I don't care what anyone says. He's *not* a backslapper."

As she wheeled Dot out to the elevator, she glanced thoughtfully down at her short, mouse-colored hair. Perhaps, unknowingly, Gwen had given Cherry another erroneous impression of the people she would be working with in this new hospital. Perhaps this mouselike child *didn't* live completely in her imagination. Her father might in some way which escaped adults really resemble the handsome Frog Prince on the ward wall. And, although a fugitive from justice, he could be sending her presents—via Mrs. Herne.

Cherry decided that she must meet Mrs. Herne at the first opportunity. She was so absorbed in her thoughts that she didn't realize she had taken the east elevator until she emerged on the second floor and found herself in the private pavilion. Cherry felt lost for a minute and stopped to orient herself outside the closed door to a private room. Which way was west where Gwen's ward was? Dorothy was babbling on:

"—and you don't *have* to mend that letter, Cherry. I've got lots of others. You can frow that torn one away."

And then the door opened and out popped a beautiful girl with a mane of shoulder-length hair, so black that it made Cherry think of a raven's wing. She burst from the room as though she had been waiting impatiently on the other side of the door for the sound of footsteps. Cherry hastily pushed Dot's wheel chair out of the way just in time to avoid a collision.

"Oh, I'm *so* sorry," Cherry cried, although she *wanted* to say: "You ought to know better than to pop out like that into a busy hospital corridor. You might have bumped into a patient on a stretcher and caused some real trouble."

The girl drew herself up haughtily and Cherry saw that she was not only beautiful but expensively well groomed from head to toe.

"Goodness gracious," she said disdainfully, "how did anyone as clumsy as you get to be a graduate nurse?"

Cherry opened her mouth to administer the scolding on the tip of her tongue, when Dot, surprisingly, flew to her defense, shouting at the top of her lungs:

"Cherry is NOT clumsy, one little bit. You're the clumsy one, Miss Slawton!"

Miss Laughton! Cherry stared. This must be the Chief's granddaughter.

Leonie Laughton stared back angrily, her full lips pouting, her dark brows puckered into an ugly scowl. She looked to Cherry so exactly like a spoiled child who will throw a tantrum before admitting she was in the wrong that Cherry decided a scolding would be a waste of breath. "Never mind, honey," Cherry said soothingly to Dot. "It doesn't matter."

At that Leonie tossed her blue-black hair and flounced back into the private room, slamming the door. Dot kicked her thin legs and yelled after her:

"Don't you ever, EVER dare call Cherry clumsy."

Cherry cradled the sobbing child in her arms, both baffled and touched by her loyalty. Baffled, because the mouselike little creature was now behaving like an angry lion cub, and yet she had displayed no emotion at all when Rudie Fowler tore up her precious letter. Then it occurred to Cherry that this might be a delayed reaction; up until now the poor little thing might have been frozen with grief.

"Don't cry, honey," she crooned. "I promised you I'd mend your letter as good as new, and I will."

Dorothy's sobs rose to a scream. "I *told* you I didn't

need that letter any more. I see my daddy most every day now, so I don't *have* to have it."

Cherry jumped, struck by the thought that perhaps the child *was*, as she kept trying to tell everyone, seeing her father—here in this hospital. *That* would explain why the letters had lost their value. And what better place could a fugitive from justice find to hide in than this big new hospital where a white coat gave him protective anonymity, and a mop and bucket the admittance card to the Medical Ward where his imaginative daughter was a patient?

Imaginative! How imaginative was Dot, anyway? She thought of herself as a mouse, but that was natural since her father called her Mouse. Was there a clue to his identity in the word frog?

"Hi, Dot." A cheery voice broke through the little girl's sobs. "What seems to be the trouble?"

A nice-looking young doctor was closing the door of a private room across the hall. He walked over to the wheel chair and held out his arms to Dot.

"We've got to snap her out of this fast, nurse," he said in a mildly critical voice to Cherry. "It's not doing her heart any good, you know."

Dot's screams subsided as she buried her face in the doctor's neck. "Cherry didn't make me cry, Al. It was Miss Slawton."

"Al," Cherry guessed, must be the other assistant

resident, Dr. Alan Dodd. He grinned over Dot's head at her and said reassuringly to the little girl:

"I told you not to let Miss Laughton upset you. She's just a butterfly. If you pay her no mind she'll always go away."

Dot giggled as he lowered her back into the wheel chair. "I forgot, Al. She looks like a beautiful black-and-gold butterfly, but she's really an ugly old pillowcase."

"Pillowcase?" Cherry was utterly confused now.

Dr. Lane threw back his head and laughed out loud. "The natural mistake of a city child. Pillowcase instead of caterpillar. But Dot's not wrong in her diagnosis. Leonie Laughton may be able to fly around on the wings of the Chief's money, but she hasn't even reached the chrysalis stage in her development yet." He stared at Cherry then, as though noticing her vivid prettiness for the first time. "I guess you're Gwen's pal, Cherry Ames?"

Cherry nodded and he held out his hand. "I'm Alan Dodd, just back from bringing some case histories down to the ENT clinic. Dave was telling me you're about the prettiest nurse he's ever seen."

Cherry flushed. "And this is just about the nicest assignment I ever had. It's all run so informally with everyone so nice and friendly. I—I *know* I'm going to love working here."

"We all do," Alan Dodd said. "And we've got Dr.

Laughton to thank for the whole setup. He thinks a children's hospital should be run efficiently, but not so efficiently that the patients feel institutionalized." He grinned. "From what I've heard about you, you're sure to fit into the Chief's scheme. I understand they had a hard time institutionalizing you when you were in training here at Spencer. I seem to remember narrow escapes involving white rabbits and demonstration dolls."

He gave Dot a friendly pat on the cheek and hurried away down the corridor. "Oh, dear," Cherry thought, "I'll never live down my old reputation."

"Al's my fav-rit doctor," Dot's voice was piping. "Next to Dave and Van. I guess Van's my very own fav-rit. He's like my daddy. You wake up and there he is sitting on your bed. And then just when you've rubbed the sleep out of your eyes, he's gone again. And Van and I play the same game my daddy and I do. I never tell Gwen or anybody when they come to see me. Not till *after*wards."

Cherry thought that through and began to understand why Gwen didn't believe the little girl when she insisted her father had brought her a present in person. And Gwen probably didn't believe her either when Dot said the quick-moving Dr. Laughton had passed through the wards.

And then Cherry made up her mind. *Jep Jepson is*

somewhere here in this hospital! He could be an orderly or an elevator man. He might be one of the workmen who were putting the finishing touches to the Contagious Ward on the floor above. He might even be employed in one of the other buildings.

"I'm going to try to solve this mystery," Cherry decided. "And the first step is to have a visit with that nice neighbor of the Jepsons, Mrs. Herne."

As though in answer to her thoughts Dot was chanting, "I'm having company this afternoon, Cherry. Mrs. 'Serne' is going to be there when I wake up from my nap. You'd better come too, Cherry. She's nice. And she knows my daddy too."

"I'll be there," Cherry promised, remembering that the ward visiting hours were from nine to ten in the morning, and from four-thirty to five-thirty in the afternoons. "I'll be there," Cherry promised.

CHAPTER V

Mrs. Herne's Testimony

AFTER HER FIRST DAY IN DR. BENHAM'S CLINIC, CHERRY felt she had learned so much that in an emergency she could give a radon treatment herself. She was both mentally and physically tired when she finally finished filing the charts. But not so tired that she wasn't looking forward to meeting Dot's friend, Mrs. Herne.

Up on the second floor she caught Gwen just returning from her two-hour rest period. Gwen was on duty from eight to six, but during the children's afternoon nap, she had two hours to herself.

"A word with you, Jones," Cherry called to her.

"A word is all I have time for," Gwen said briskly.

"Well, in a word then," Cherry began with a giggle, and hurriedly told Gwen her suspicions that Dot Jepson's father might be working somewhere at Spencer.

Gwen tapped her forehead sadly, indicating that Cherry had lost her mind. "Dot's hypnotized you, Ames. If anyone faintly resembling a Frog Prince came in here, I'd know about it. No matter what disguise he wore."

"I'm not so sure of that," Cherry said slowly. But Gwen wasn't listening. She was smiling at a plump, freckle-faced woman who had just emerged from the visitors' elevator.

"Hello, Mrs. Herne," she greeted her. "Dot's been counting the minutes ever since she got your postcard."

"Well, and so have I," the cheerful woman said. "I miss the little tyke—she was like one of my own, Miss Jones, and my heart aches to think that I can't take her home with me when she's ready to go."

"We all feel the same way," Gwen said. "This is Miss Cherry Ames, Mrs. Herne. She's already fallen in love with Dot."

Cherry shook hands with the plump lady and said, "I was just going in to visit her, but you go first. I know how busy you are, and I can see her every day when I'm off duty."

Mrs. Herne's broad face crinkled into a grin of delight. "Well, now, Miss Cherry, I guess you're busy too, but if you could just pop in for a minute or two every now and then I wouldn't worry so much. The poor lamb misses her father so badly! I declare, after I've had a talk with her I go right home and have a good long cry. She's a brave little thing, that's what she is, pretendin' now that he comes to see her and brings her presents. She just does that, you know, so the rest of us won't guess how much she aches for him deep down inside." She handed Gwen her visitor's admittance card, and hurried down the corridor to the ward. Gwen and Cherry followed more slowly.

Cherry sat in a chair beside Gwen's desk and watched Dot delightedly hug and kiss her visitor. Then Mrs. Herne's broad back cut off the rest of the scene in Dot's glass cubicle. Cherry was thinking:

"Mrs. Herne is too honest and sincere to act out a lie. She really agrees with Gwen that Dot's pretending, so that means she hasn't any idea where Jep Jepson is hiding."

After a minute Gwen came back from her inspection of the ward and said, "You don't have to sit here, Cherry. Dot and Mrs. Herne haven't got any secrets. Why don't you join them? They're cutting out paper dolls from that book Dot claims her father brought her early this morning."

Cherry stared at Gwen across the desk. "If he didn't bring it to her, who did?"

Gwen shrugged. "I haven't the faintest idea. It was

there when I came on duty at eight. Anybody could have salvaged it from one of the private rooms on any floor. Those rich kids often leave behind stuff their parents or nurses can't cram into their suitcases when they're discharged. That rocking horse over there, for instance, is a little something Dave Lane salvaged from Surgical last week."

"A rocking horse is one thing," Cherry said stubbornly. "And a paper-doll book another."

Gwen chuckled. "A horse of a different size, you mean? All right, Ames, have it your own way. There's an escaped convict lurking around here. So now I know it's he who swipes the leftover desserts, not Polly Probie."

Cherry tossed her black curls and started across the huge linoleum checkerboard on the floor. As she entered Dot's cubicle, Mrs. Herne looked up with a guilty expression on her freckled face. Dot was licking the last drop from a tiny ice cream container.

"Oh, now I've done it," Mrs. Herne moaned. "You've caught me in the act, Miss Cherry. I know the children have ice cream three times a week, and I shouldn't have brought her anythin' to eat so near her suppertime. But I racked my brains, I'm tellin' you, Miss Cherry. What else could I buy with the six cents that I save, a penny a day, from my food money?"

Cherry sat on the other side of Dot's bed. "You

couldn't have bought anything she enjoyed more, Mrs. Herne," she said with a smile. "And ice cream is good for convalescent children. I'm sure it won't spoil your appetite for supper, will it, Dot?"

"Course not," Dot said airily and pushed some cutouts across the blanket toward Cherry. "See? I told my daddy I wanted some pretty ladies with lots of pretty dresses, and that's just what he brought me the minute I woke up this morning. My daddy's just about the smartest man in the whole wide world."

Mrs. Herne gave Cherry a significant glance which said more plainly than words, "Dreamin', she was, of course, the poor lamb." Later, when the visiting hour was over, Cherry went out in the corridor with Mrs. Herne.

As they waited for the elevator, she said, "I know you're in a hurry to get home, Mrs. Herne, but I wish you could tell me something about Dot's father. I mean, about the robbery and the trial, and what *you* really think happened that night."

For the second time that day Mrs. Herne looked at Cherry with a guilty expression on her face. "I'd like to talk to you about it," she said. "I'd like to—to unburden my soul, Miss Cherry. I just can't seem to get it out of mind that it's all my fault that poor man was sent to jail." She glanced apprehensively over her shoulder at the other visitors who had gathered around the elevator. "Is there any place where we can go and talk without anyone listenin' to my—my—" She laughed nervously. "My confession?"

Cherry said quickly, "The big waiting room on the main floor. It'll be empty now that visiting hours are over for the day. Come on." She was too excited to wait for the elevator, and grabbing the woman's plump, perspiring hand, tugged her impatiently across the hall and down the stairs. Once they were seated together on a black leather settee in the comforting semidarkness of the deserted waiting room, Mrs. Herne did indeed "unburden her soul" to Cherry.

"It was that prosecutin' attorney, Miss Cherry," she blurted. "He kept hammerin' and hammerin' at me. Would I swear on the Bible that Jep had been gone only long enough to buy that aspirin and come right back? At first I did swear that he hadn't been gone long enough to buy the aspirin and break into the pawnshop on the same block too. But then when they told me that Dot herself had said her daddy had been gone a long, long time, I broke down, Miss Cherry. I don't know how long it takes a man to smash a window and snatch up some jewels and a watch. And I didn't even look at the clock when I sent Jep out after the aspirin. So how could I be sure, Miss Cherry?"

It was as though she were begging Cherry not to hate her for telling the truth on the witness stand, and Cherry said soothingly, "Of course, you couldn't be absolutely sure, Mrs. Herne. But please begin at the very beginning. You see, I don't know anything about the case."

Gradually Cherry got the whole story. Jep, down to his last cent, discouraged because he was jobless, but even more discouraged because his Mouse was growing no better, had stepped across the hall and tapped on Mrs. Herne's door.

"Please, Meg," he had said. "I'm worried about Dot. Her face is so red, and her eyes so bright, and her thin little wrists are puffed up like balloons. Could you come over a minute and take a look at her?"

Meg Herne had taken one look at the sick little girl and, without benefit of a thermometer, had known she had at least two degrees of fever. She told Jep not to worry, that she would notify Miss Gardner, the visiting nurse, in the morning. In the meantime she improvised an ice bag and sent Jep out for a small bottle of aspirin.

"He couldn't have been gone more than ten minutes, Miss Cherry," she said. "I had barely time to hurry across the hall for a chunk of ice, stick it in the toe of an old, clean sock, and smash it with my iron before Jep was back. All out of breath, he was, but proud that he'd had just enough money left to pay for the aspirin himself. A proud man, Jep Jepson, never liked to ask help from anyone, and earnin' good money too, until Dot got so she wouldn't eat unless he coaxed her and fed her with a spoon. It was then he gave up his good job and began workin' as a night watchman." Her big shoulders heaved. "Burnin' the candle at both ends, Miss Cherry. It never works. I warned him, but he loves that child so, he just can't listen to reason."

Cherry said quietly, "Do you yourself believe, Mrs. Herne, that Jep broke into the pawnshop?"

Meg Herne stared down at her big, work-worn hands. "I don't know what to believe, Miss Cherry. He was a proud man, as I keep tellin' you, and the sight of those jewels and that big gold watch must have been mighty temptin'. I don't know but what I might have been tempted myself if I'd been in his shoes. Me with ten mouths to feed, and suppose Jerry Herne didn't turn over his pay envelope to me every Friday night?"

"I know just what you mean," Cherry said sympathetically. "But Jep could have got another job, couldn't he?"

"That he could," Mrs. Herne said emphatically. "And one where he could have kept an eye on Dot at the same time too. As the super of our three buildings. I was just about to write to the owner myself and suggest in

plain language that he fire that lazy, good-for-nothin'
super we have now and hire Jep in his place. He would
have done it too, the owner, for he knows me from way
back. All nine of my children were born there in No. 27
Duele Street, Miss Cherry, and I don't miss much that
goes on in No. 29 or No. 25 either, you can be sure.
More than once the owner has asked my advice about
who should be evicted and who should be allowed to
stay on for a breathin' spell between jobs even after the
rent was long overdue."

Cherry could not suppress a smile. "I'll bet you run
the whole neighborhood, Mrs. Herne," she said. "But
there's one thing you couldn't possibly know, and that
is that the doctors here have just discovered that Dot is
a little hard of hearing. Don't you see what that means?
When the police detectives questioned her she may not
have heard everything they said. She may have told
them her father *did* leave her for a long, long time,
meaning that he did during the time that he was a night
watchman."

Mrs. Herne clasped her forehead with both calloused
hands. "Oh, my goodness gracious, Miss Cherry, that's
just the way it was. Now, Calahan, the cop on our beat,
he's the nicest young lad you'd ever like to meet, and
not wantin' for one minute to have Jep sent off to prison.
So he asks Dot as gently as could be, 'Now, honey, when

your daddy went off and left you with Mrs. Herne while he went around the corner, was he gone for a long, long time, or just a minute or two?' And the poor lamb was thinkin' of the nights when Jep, leavin' for work, would leave her door ajar so I could hear her if she called. He would say, 'Mouse, I'm going to be gone for a long, long time. So you try hard to sleep until I come back.' Oh, Miss Cherry, I should have remembered, all that, but somehow, when that lawyer began hammerin' at me, I forgot everythin', even my own name!"

Cherry bit her lip. She knew she had a long way to go before she could prove her growing suspicion that Jep had been unjustly albeit, without malice, convicted on the testimony of his own daughter! The whole question of his guilt might have hung on the one phrase that Dot probably hadn't heard—the phrase "while he went around the corner" in the question which began, "When your Daddy went off and left you with Mrs. Herne . . ."

Cherry could see it all in her imagination: the friendly patrolman, Calahan, lowering his voice sympathetically as the detectives took notes, and not one of them knowing that the child was slightly deaf. And the child, remembering only the recent nights when Jep had left her for a long, long time, answering emphatically. Mrs. Herne, bewildered and perspiring on the

witness stand, breaking down under the too-often repeated questions of the State's attorney. And the dis-
interested, State-appointed counsel for the defense,
listening boredly instead of cross-examining the witnesses who testified against the client he took for
granted was guilty.

"Something has to be done about all this," Cherry
said, getting up suddenly. "I don't think Dot's father
committed that robbery any more than you do, Mrs.
Herne. As soon as I find out more about the case, may
I call on your help?"

"That you can." Mrs. Herne, after one glance at the
waiting room clock, began to waddle hurriedly out to
the lobby. "No. 27 Duele Street is where I live, Miss
Cherry, but everyone on the block knows me, in case
you forget."

Cherry strolled after her toward the entrance thinking this might be a good time to say "hello" to the red-
headed doorman. And then she remembered that his
hours were from eight to four as were hers. She also remembered that the Spencer bus which transported hospital visitors to and from the main city bus stop had
probably already gone, leaving poor Mrs. Herne faced
with a long walk through the hospital grounds and down
the hill. She broke into a run, planning to ask the doorman on duty to signal for a cab which Cherry would

pay for herself. But with a sigh of relief she saw that the bus was just pulling out of the driveway.

Mrs. Herne stuck her face out of an open window and yelled to Cherry: "Be good to my Dot. Try and visit her whenever you can."

Cherry nodded and waved. As the bus roared away, a shiny, maroon roadster careened around it to come to a stop in a swirl of gravel in front of the hospital. Cherry frowned. The owner of that expensive-looking car had no business driving so fast on hospital grounds.

The driver, Cherry saw at once, was Leonie Laughton who fretfully blew her horn until the doorman hurried down the steps in answer. "I'm waiting for Dr. David Lane," Cherry heard her say in her disdainful, affected voice. "We're late. Please tell him to hurry."

The doorman politely tipped his cap and started toward the outside phone booth. And then Cherry heard someone come out of the big swinging door behind her. A pleasant, masculine voice said teasingly:

"Hello, Miss Ames. Are you assisting the doorman now? Didn't we work you hard enough in the clinic today?"

Cherry wheeled to face him. "Oh, hello, Dr. Lane. No, I'm not assisting anyone. Just sort of getting oriented."

There was something more than the mere friendly

camaraderie of hospital teammates in his blue eyes as he said quietly, "We're not on duty now, you know. You *could* call me David without making anybody mad."

And then someone *did* call him David, in a high-pitched, spoiled-child voice. "Day-*vid!*" Leonie Laughton's pretty face was twisted with impatience—or, perhaps, Cherry couldn't help thinking—jealousy. "Day-vid! For heaven's sake, the party began at five. If you're going to stand there talking to that nurse all day we might as well give up the whole idea."

A dark flush spread over Dr. Lane's handsome features and for a minute Cherry thought he was going to make an angry retort. Then he slowly unclenched his taut hands and walked down the steps.

Cherry stared after the maroon roadster until it sped around the bend in the driveway. "Whew!" she said to no one in particular. "I've got another mystery on my hands. David Lane doesn't admire Leonie Laughton any more than anyone else around here does. And yet, as Gwen hinted last night, he certainly obeys her as though he were her trick bear with a ring in his nose!"

CHAPTER VI

~~~~~~~~~~~~~~~~~~~~~~~~~~~~

The Lane-Laughton Matter

CHERRY WALKED BACK INTO THE LOBBY OF CHILDREN'S and down the steps to the tunnel leading to Crowley. Hurrying toward her from the other direction were Gwen and Josie.

"We were just coming to get you," Gwen said. "How did you make out with Mrs. Herne? You left my floor as thick as two thieves!"

"I'll tell you all about that after dinner," Cherry said. "But right now what mystifies me is why a marvelous young doctor like David Lane wastes his time dancing attendance on a spoiled deb like Leonie Laughton."

Gwen shrugged. "I told you what the gossip on that is, Cherry. David thinks that beauing the Chief's granddaughter around is going to get him the Residency."

"I don't believe it," Cherry said stanchly. "The people who claim David is a backslapper are just jealous of his ability. I've worked with him all day, Gwen, and I think he's one of the most intelligent, understanding, and able doctors I've ever known."

"I agree with you," Gwen said. "And I also agree with you that Dr. Laughton is going to give out that appointment on merit alone. In which case I'm pretty sure David will be our next Resident."

Cherry frowned. "What worries me is that the best man may not win after all. Dr. Laughton has already heard the rumor that David is a politician. The Chief doesn't strike me as the type of man who could be influenced by idle gossip, but he may feel that where there's smoke there's bound to be fire."

Arm in arm, they strolled back to Crowley and Gwen said soberly, "I see what you're driving at, Ames. None of us can understand what David sees in Leonie. Her grandfather has been heard to refer to her as that flibbertigibbet more than once. Therefore he, too, must suspect that there's a method in David's apparent madness."

"Of course," Josie put in matter-of-factly, "it may not be madness. It may be an infatuation. From the glimpse I had of her today, Leonie struck me as being pretty glamorous."

"That must be it," Cherry agreed, furiously daubing white polish on her shoes. "And the sad part of it is that the gossip can't be squelched until David stops being infatuated. By that time it may be too late."

Josie laughed. "In my opinion, David is already on the road to recovery. You haven't got eyes in the back of your head," she told Cherry, "so you couldn't see what I saw all day long. Every time David Lane held the treatment-room door open for you when you brought in a patient he looked as if he were singing:

" *'You've got the sweetest face in all the world,*
And I want you for my girl—'"

Cherry collapsed on her bed, helpless with laughter. "You're wonderful, Josie," she cried, "especially since the girl in that song had yellow hair and big blue eyes."

"I don't care," Josie interrupted stubbornly. "The rest of it *does* describe you, and how David Lane feels about you."

Gwen said tartly, her blue eyes twinkling, "When you two are through making idiots of yourselves, I'd like to say a little something."

Cherry sat up. "Speak, my old friend," she said. "And don't think you can hurt my feelings. You made it quite clear last night that even if I wanted to I couldn't cure David of his infatuation for Leonie."

"That's what I said last night," Gwen admitted. "But

now I'm beginning to think that our two assistant residents may be rivals in more ways than one. I wish you could have heard Alan Dodd raving about you when I went off duty this afternoon. He cornered me just as I was tottering into the elevator.

" 'What's the idea of holding out on us, Gwen?' he demanded. 'Where've you been keeping that pretty red-cheeked friend of yours?' " Gwen sighed tiredly. "It went on like that for what seemed to me like hours."

Cherry slid off the bed. "Enough of this foolishness, girls. I'm starving."

"And I," Gwen said, "want to know why you think there's an escaped convict disguised as a frog bouncing around on my floor."

"A frog?" Josie exploded. "What next? Have you both lost your minds?"

"A frog *prince*," Cherry said, and explained.

Josie's eyes widened behind her glasses and she grabbed Cherry's wrist, pretending to be very much interested in finding her pulse. "She's in her second childhood," she told Gwen, with mock melancholy. "Have you an extra bed on your ward?"

Cherry, suppressing a giggle, said as sternly as possible, "Please stop clowning, you two. I've got very good reasons to suspect that Jep Jepson is employed somewhere at Spencer. Furthermore, after talking with Dot's friend, Mrs. Herne, I'm beginning to suspect that Jep didn't commit that robbery!"

This bombshell sobered Gwen and Josie very quickly. Throughout dinner they listened without interrupting as she repeated her conversation with Mrs. Herne.

"Don't you see?" she finished. "The whole case hinged on Mrs. Herne's testimony which was broken down by Dot's. And nobody knew a month ago that Dot was hard of hearing."

Someone poked Cherry in the back then and she jumped, almost upsetting her coffee. "I don't know what you're talking about, Ames," a voice said. "But I'm not hard of hearing, and I could recognize your Illinois twang across the room."

Cherry twisted around to stare up into the smiling face of the pretty nurse who had been in charge of Ward 4, Cherry's and Josie's first assignment as probationers.

"Miss Baker!" Cherry and Josie yelled in unison.

"Mrs. Jim Clayton, you mean." The golden-haired young woman held up her left hand, proudly displaying her wedding ring. "But please call me Marjory. I know you always did behind my back when you were probies." She yanked an empty chair from a near-by table and joined their group. "Jim is a resident over at City Hospital," she explained, "so I decided to stay right on at Spencer until he's ready to go into private practice."

Cherry smiled, remembering the tall, dark young doctor who had been an intern when she started in training. "Give Jim my very best," she said when Marjory Baker Clayton was called back to her own table. "If it hadn't been for him, I would have been expelled for borrowing Sally Chase."

Marjory's hazel eyes twinkled. "That was nothing to the really big scrape you two got involved in. Remember that midnight emergency operation in the forbidden room?"

"I'll never forget it," Cherry called after her, and turned back to Gwen and Josie. "She's prettier than ever, isn't she?"

"And lucky to have a profession," Josie said practically. "It isn't everybody who can afford to marry a resident. Present company excluded of course," she teased. "Now you and rich little Leonie—"

"Oh, stop it, Franklin." Cherry pushed back her chair and jumped impulsively to her feet. "Let's forget about the Lane-Laughton matter and concentrate on finding out who *did* commit that pawnshop robbery."

Without comment they followed her out into the yard, and Cherry told them, "Tomorrow, as soon as I get off duty, I'm going to the *News* and get permission from the editor to read all the clippings on the Jepson case they must have on file in their morgue."

"That's a good idea," Gwen said approvingly. "You'll surely get more clues."

"I doubt that," Josie said. "It certainly wasn't important enough to have made the front pages."

Cherry bit her lip impatiently. "Of course the robbery didn't make the front page," she said briskly. "But when Jep escaped from prison all of the papers must have carried a description of him. And that's where you two come in. Once we know what he looks like, you girls have got to keep an eye out for him."

Josie sighed. "An Ames convinced against her will is of the same opinion still," she chanted. "But have it your own way, honey. I hereby swear that all the male employees on the main floor, whether they're disguised as mice, men or frogs, are Jep Jepson until proved otherwise."

They were back in Cherry's room now, and Gwen stretched out on the bed, cupping her chin in the palm of her hand thoughtfully. "I'll sign on that dotted line too," she said. "*After* you've solved the mystery, Cherry."

Cherry's black eyes widened. "Oh, Gwen," she moaned, "I never thought about that. If we find out he's working at Spencer as an elevator boy or an orderly or something, we'd have to turn him over to the police, wouldn't we?" Then she added triumphantly, "That is, if I haven't found out first who the real criminal is."

Gwen yawned and stretched. "Let's not worry about that now. The thing for you to do is to get more clues, and you can count on Josie and me to help in any way we can."

Cherry impulsively hugged them both. "Then that makes us all triplets in crime, accessories after the fact, I guess a lawyer would call us."

Gwen unconcernedly ran her hands through her short red hair. "Well, facts are what we want, Ames, and after that a good lawyer. If you solve this mystery, you'll be solving all of Dot's problems too. I'd do almost anything to make sure that when she's discharged she'll go home to her own father." She squeezed Cherry's hand affectionately. "We're counting on you, Ames, and *you* can count on us to the bitter end."

"That's right," Josie said, and added cautiously, "But don't let the end be too bitter. What I mean is, don't get yourself into a dangerous situation, Cherry. We aren't sure yet that Dot's father *didn't* commit the crime. An escaped convict when cornered might be—well, down-right dangerous."

"I second that motion," Gwen said heartily. "Once you prove Jep *is* innocent, Cherry, let the police track down the real crook."

"I'll be good," Cherry promised, and held the door of her room open invitingly. "Now scram, girls. I've got a long hard day ahead of me tomorrow."

And a long, hard day it turned out to be. It was six o'clock when Cherry came out of the newspaper office and stood on the street wondering where she could get a quick cup of hot tea. She was exhausted and thirsty and she wanted to sit down somewhere and immediately make a list of the clues she had collected from the *News* files.

People were hurrying out of the huge office buildings all around her, and not one of them seemed to care whether she proved Jep Jepson's innocence or not. Cherry felt lost and alone and wished that she could somehow sprout wings that would take her right back to her friends at Crowley. And then someone touched her arm, and she looked up into David Lane's smiling face.

"Kind of far from home, aren't you, Cherry Ames?" he asked.

Cherry smiled back at him. "Well, so are you, David Lane. Not that it's any of my business, but what have you been doing in the *News* offices this afternoon?"

He guided her through the crowd to a gay little tea-room. "I could ask you the same question," he said when they had given the waitress their order of tea and cinnamon toast. "But I'll be polite and answer yours first. I'm working with a reporter who's going to write a series on the subject of diabetes in young children. The early symptoms are so easily mistaken for something else that by the time the kids are brought to us they're often in really bad shape. I've at last convinced my reporter friend that the public ought to be told more about insulin, and he, in turn, has just convinced his managing editor that a series of articles packed with actual case histories would not only be interesting but informative."

Cherry glanced at his serious young face and said softly, "You have the same crusading spirit that Dr. Benham has. Are you going to specialize in diabetics?"

He frowned. "No, although in a way I'd like to. No," he said again, so firmly that Cherry suspected he might be trying to convince himself of his ambition. "No, I'm going to be a pediatrician, a *topflight* pediatrician, Cherry Ames. I don't care how how long it takes me to get to the top of the ladder, but I'm going to get there." He banged a big fist on the glass-topped table until the silverware jumped and clattered in protest. "I saw my father bury himself and his talents in a small town," he almost shouted, "and I'm not going to follow in his footsteps. What kind of life does a country doctor lead, anyway?"

"A very wonderful and satisfying life," Cherry said quietly. "A country doctor's talents are not limited to his profession. He is not only a physician, but he's generally a friend and advisor and often as not a father-confessor to most of the people in his community. I can't imagine having any ambition higher than that."

"Well, *I* can," David retorted. "Without any false modesty, Cherry, I'll tell you right now that I'm a good doctor, one of the best in my field. I wouldn't be where I am today if I wasn't. But do you think I'm going to let things stop here on this rung of the ladder? Sure, I'm Assistant Resident of the Children's General Hospital, and that's something, but not enough. I want to keep climbing until I reach the very top. I want to be as famous someday as—as Dr. Van Laughton!"

Cherry waited until the waitress had unloaded her tray of dishes and gone away. She stirred sugar in her cup of steaming tea and said thoughtfully, "I can understand your wanting to be as great a man as Dr. Laughton, David. But a great man doesn't necessarily have to be famous, does he?"

The hot color in David's flushed face faded and then came rushing back again. "Oh, I know what you're driving at," he admitted finally, rather shamefacedly, Cherry thought. "But don't you see? Van Laughton is both great *and* famous. I want to be just like him."

"I don't blame you." Cherry smiled. "But aren't you going about it the wrong way? From what our own country doctor, Dr. Joe Fortune, told me about the Chief, I gather that he climbed rather slowly to the top, taking each rung at a time, and didn't waste a minute worrying about how the world was going to look after he'd climbed up all the way."

David suddenly threw back his head and roared with laughter. "Oh, for heaven's sake," he groaned, "you sound just like my old man. And you resemble him about as much as Dot Jepson resembles the fat lady in the circus. The kids back home call Dad Santa Claus."

"He sounds like a very cheerful—*and* a very happy person," Cherry pointed out.

"He is," David admitted. "All right, why don't you go ahead and say it? Why don't you ask me why I waste my time taking Leonie Laughton to dull parties?"

"Why do you?" Cherry said quietly.

He carefully squeezed a lemon slice into his tea, avoiding her eyes. "She's not a bad kid, Cherry, just spoiled as any only child usually is," he said. "And she thinks she's in love with me. At first I felt sorry for her, that's why I accepted the invitation to her coming-out party. After that, seeing her became more or less of a habit. Then when she got fired as a nurse's aide, I couldn't very well break off taking her around at that time. It would have looked as though I quit seeing her because she was in disgrace."

"I understand," Cherry said sympathetically. "It *is* rather tough on you, being the man in this case, isn't it? You don't want to be discourteous or hurt her feelings, and yet you don't want to let her think you're in love with her if you're not." She finished carefully, "You *aren't* in love with her, are you?"

He stopped with his cup half way to his mouth and the tea slopped out into his saucer. "Good gosh, no! And even if I were I wouldn't let her know it. It'll be years before I can afford to get married, as you well know, Cherry." His big shoulders shook with laughter. "Imagine Leonie Laughton living on an assistant resident's pittance! Why, I couldn't even buy gas for her high-powered car."

Cherry laughed with him and then sobered. "Seriously, though, David, in all fairness, you ought to let Leonie know how you feel about her—and marriage."

"I know it," he said ruefully. "But somehow I can't. She's such a kid and I keep hoping somebody in her own crowd will fall in love with her and make her forget all about me. Frankly," he went on, "I think she's in love with the idea that I'm a doctor, not with me.

You know, the white coat, and the hospital, and the siren of an ambulance screaming up to the place. They all seem pretty glamorous to an outsider."

"They still seem pretty glamorous to me," Cherry said, smiling. "But I know what you mean. Leonie might find out too late that she wouldn't like being married to a doctor. But she should know that as often as not when she's all dressed for a party you might be called out on an emergency case."

He nodded. "I can't seem to get the idea through her pretty little head. While I'm a resident of course I have more or less regular hours, but later on I won't. She was too young to remember when her grandfather was in private practice." He paid the check and helped Cherry into the jacket of her trim tweed suit.

"Then Leonie's father isn't a physician?" she asked.

"No. According to Leonie he gave up the idea after a year of pre-med. Wanted to do something on his own, not be borne aloft on his father's reputation. I can understand that. If Dad had been famous, I'd probably be practicing law right now."

Cherry laughed. "I doubt that. My guess is that you would have ended up a doctor no matter what your father's profession had been."

He followed her through the revolving door and they stood there for a minute in the cold October twilight.

"Don't pay attention to me when I'm in one of my moods, Cherry," he said suddenly. "It's my standard repartee when the interns kid me about Leonie at chow. I can't come right out and tell them that she's just a kid who thinks she's in love with me and I'm trying to talk her out of it. Al understands, but the interns are such kids themselves they don't get it."

"Alan Dodd," Cherry said thoughtfully, "does understand. Yesterday he said Leonie was still in the chrysalis stage of her development, implying, I guess, that when she finally grows up she'll be all right. He seems like an awfully nice person, David. How does he feel about the Residency?"

David shrugged. "I honestly don't think he cares if he gets it or not, Cherry. He keeps saying I'm the right man for it—that he doesn't like the kind of responsibility that goes with it. Naturally, he wouldn't turn it down, but if he doesn't get it, my guess is that he'll join forces with our present Resident when he starts private practice next year." He clenched his big hands. "And I—I *do* want to be topflight, Cherry, but I've got a long, long way to go."

"Then actually," Cherry said soberly, "you want the Residency because you want the additional training that goes with it. That's your problem, isn't it?"

He hailed a cab for her and put her in it. "Not my

only problem," he said with a rueful grin. "If you get any bright ideas on how I can cure Leonie of her infatuation for me without hurting her feelings, let me know, won't you?"

Cherry waved good-bye, smiling to herself. "I haven't a bright idea at the moment, but something's sure to happen that'll cure Leonie and convince her grandfather that David is the right man for the post."

She leaned back in the seat, closing her eyes as the cab started up the hill to Spencer. Inside her handbag were pages of notes she had scribbled down from the *News* files on the Jepson case.

Cherry could hardly wait to discuss her new clues with Gwen and Josie.

CHAPTER VII

The Mysterious Mr. X

GWEN AND JOSIE WERE WAITING FOR HER WHEN
Cherry got back to her room at Crowley. Gwen was
perched on the window seat, Josie was curled up on the
bed, and they both were munching huge slices of choc-
olate cake.

"You missed second dinner," Gwen said, "but it
doesn't matter. This delicious cake just arrived in that
box over there on your bureau. It was marked 'Handle
with Care—PERISHABLE!' So we decided that the
best way to take care of it was to eat it." She giggled
and almost choked on a crumb. "Hope you don't mind."

"Perish the thought," Cherry said, reading the label.
The return address was:

"Miss Margaret Fortune, Hilton, Illinois."

Cherry gasped. "It's from Midge."

Gwen screamed and wrapped her arms around her stomach, pretending to writhe in agony. "Help, I've been poisoned! Is there a doctor in the house?"

Josie joined in the act. "Call an ambulance! Get a stomach pump! Oh, Cherry, if Midge baked that cake the label should have read: *'Eat* with Care. PTO-MAINE!'"

Tears of laughter streamed from Cherry's dark eyes, then suddenly they were tears of homesickness. She missed her young-looking, sweet-faced mother, the most understanding mother in the world. And her tall father with his businesslike stride and warm, friendly smile. *And* her keen-eyed twin brother, Charlie, who teased her unmercifully but affectionately.

Cherry could almost see Dr. Joe's little white frame cottage with its topsy-turvy interior, for his teen-age daughter, Midge, was not a housekeeper in any sense of the word.

"Midge Fortune," Cherry said, without realizing that she was thinking out loud, "can't boil water without burning it. Who in the world could have baked this yummy-looking cake?"

"Ho-hum," Gwen said, reaching for another slice. "Why don't you read the card that was enclosed with it?"

Cherry shook her finger under Gwen's pert nose. "You bad girl! Reading other people's mail!"

Josie rushed to Gwen's defense. "We didn't do anything of the sort. See?" She pointed to a small white envelope tucked in a corner of Cherry's mirror. On it was written:

"For Cherry. To be shared with Gwen and Josie."

Cherry read the enclosed card out loud:

"Dear Cherry, Happy homecoming back to Spencer! Midge spent the weekend with us and is going to mail this to you from the station on her way home. She helped me bake it—that is she cracked the eggs, so forgive the shells! Love, Bertha."

"Well, no wonder it's divine," Cherry said, scooping up a piece of icing from the waxed paper. "Bertha's a wonderful cook. And that fiend, Midge, not knowing about the card, hoped she could fool us into thinking she baked it."

"She didn't fool me," Gwen said, licking her lips. "I saw the New York postmark and guessed it was from No. 9. What a time the gang must have had with Midge as a weekend guest! How do you suppose that happened?"

"I think I can guess," Cherry said. "When I was home, before reporting for duty here, Dr. Joe told me he might have to fly to New York for a medical conference. Guess he decided to take Midge along as a treat."

"You mean," Josie put in, "because he didn't dare leave her behind! You've got more mail, Cherry. Do you want to read it before you tell us what you discovered in the *News* files about the Jepson case?"

"We-ell, if you don't mind," Cherry said and picked up a card addressed in Charlie's strong, masculine handwriting:

"Hi, honey! I'll be home for the Halloween weekend. Can you make it too? Bring Gwen and Josie and we'll have a house party complete with pumpkin pie and popcorn."

And there was a short note from Cherry's mother repeating the invitation: "Dad and I do hope you all can come, darling. Bring along any of your old or new friends you'd like to ask. We can put up extra cots in your room and Charlie's. Write soon, but not if you're too tired or too busy."

"Isn't that just like my mother?" Cherry demanded. "As if I'd ever be too tired or too busy to write *her!*"

"She's a wonderful person all right," Gwen agreed. "And I sure do hope we have that weekend off so we can accept her invitation to the house party."

"Me too." Josie snatched up a little framed calendar on Cherry's desk. "Let's see. Is Halloween the last Thursday in the month, or is that Thanksgiving?"

"Josie!" Cherry scolded her. "You don't deserve an R.N. after your name. Thanksgiving is the last Thursday in *November*, and Halloween, which is the night before All Saints' Day, is the last day in October."

"I never can keep them straight in my mind," Josie admitted with a laugh. "But one thing I do know is that my boss told me today that there's not going to be any clinic on Saturday, October thirty-first. Which, according to your expert calculations, is Halloween."

"Which," Gwen finished with a groan, "means you two will be in Hilton then, while I'll probably be stuck here without even a jack-o'-lantern to keep me company."

"Oh, Gwen," Cherry cried sympathetically. "Can't you arrange it somehow? Switch with the night nurse or something?"

"Um-m-m," Gwen said, as though trying to make up her mind. "Yes, I guess it would be worth it in this particular case. No price is too high to pay for a weekend at the Ameses."

"Why, what's the matter with you, Jones?" Cherry demanded. "Since when did you develop such an aversion to night duty?"

"It's not the duty," Gwen told her. "It's the Night Supervisor. She's a wonderful nurse, mind you, and I have all the respect in the world for her executive ability. But, golly, is she ever a stiff-necked martinet! Celine, the girl who relieves me at night, you know, said that Mrs. Welch is like the Chief in that she's everywhere at once and never misses a trick. Woe betide the nurse who meets with her disapproval!"

Josie let out a long sigh. "Thank goodness I'll never have to run into her. We're lucky, aren't we, Cherry?"

"Yes and no," Cherry said, thinking it through. "As a matter of fact, my secret ambition is to be a night supervisor sometime. It must be a wonderful and thrilling experience to be in full charge of a whole hospital at night with all the doctors away or asleep."

"Well, you can have it," Josie said emphatically. "Me, I just couldn't take that much responsibility. And I can understand why anyone that does has to be pretty much of a martinet."

"I can too." Cherry nodded. "A tiny breach of discipline might throw a monkey wrench into the whole machinery."

Gwen chuckled. "You may be a night supervisor someday, Ames, but you'll never be stiff-necked. And to get back to the matter under discussion, I happen to know that Celine would like to switch with me on Friday, the thirtieth. She wants to go to her sister's wedding that night. So I'll swap on the condition that she pinch-hits for me the next day."

"Wonderful," Cherry cried. "I'll write Mother right away that we'll be there."

"No, you won't," Gwen interrupted. "That comes later. Right now, Josie and I are dying of curiosity. Did you find any clues in the clips at the *News* morgue?"

With a mysterious expression on her pretty face, Cherry sat down at her desk and opened her handbag. It had been fairly bursting with her notes and now they popped out on the red blotter as though they couldn't stand being suppressed another minute. Gwen, from her perch on the window seat, scooped up one page as it fluttered temptingly in her direction.

"Having committed the crime of opening your package and reading half of your mail," she said mischievously, "I shall now try to decipher your shorthand, Ames. Um-m-m, let's see now, what do you use, Gregg or Pitman?"

"Neither," Cherry said, snatching the sheet of paper away from Gwen. "You were holding it upside down, silly." She sobered. "Let's get down to business, girls. This is a serious matter. I'm surer than ever now that Jep Jepson is innocent."

Josie wriggled closer so that she could watch Cherry's face from the bed. "Begin at the beginning, please," she begged. "Who, where, when, what, and why?"

"The who is still an unknown quantity," Cherry told her. "A mysterious Mr. X, who, I am convinced, looks enough like Jep so that several bystanders mistook the real criminal for him. Jep, you see, is tall and thin, slightly stoop-shouldered, and has prematurely white hair. Any other man of the same build and who was also wearing blue jeans that evening, but who had very *blond* hair, might have been mistaken for Jep as he darted under the street light and into the tenement."

"Which brings you to the where," Gwen put in.

"That's right." Cherry consulted her notes. "We've all been visiting nurses so we know what the poorer section of a big city looks like. Jep and Dot lived in a tenement, No. 27 Duele Street. About a five-minute walk away, around the corner on broad West Avenue, is the neighborhood drugstore, Palin's. The pawnshop, which was robbed, is next door to Palin's. There wasn't much of value on display. Some jewelry, totaling in value not more than five hundred dollars, and a big gold watch which nobody except the owner of the pawn ticket would want because of the distinctive monogram on the back."

Cherry tilted back in her chair so she could look at both Gwen and Josie. "Don't forget about that watch. It's important. The initials were—or, I should say, *are*, H. T. A."

"How did you find that out?" Josie demanded suspiciously. "Surely the robbery wasn't important enough for the papers to run a detailed description of every stolen item."

"Of course not," Cherry admitted. "The only reason why it received the publicity it did was that court was in session at the time of the robbery and so the trial and conviction followed almost immediately upon its heels. All nicely timed so that the newspapers could point up the efficiency of our police force. The crime itself was reported in a brief item, but the trial took up a lot more space." She sighed. "If it had taken a lot more time, or had been delayed until the next session, Jep might have had a chance."

"I imagine it was a pretty cut-and-dried affair," Gwen said shrewdly. "With a State-appointed counsel for the defense?"

"That's right," Cherry said. "So now you've got the who, the where, and the what. The when is also very important. There can be no doubt that the pawnshop was broken into sometime between nine and nine-thirty. The officer on the beat, Calahan, passes the pawnshop every half hour as he makes his evening rounds. When he passed it at nine on the dot, the window was not broken, but when he passed it again at nine-thirty, it was. Shortly before he discovered the glass on the sidewalk, he had noticed someone hurrying around the corner into Duele Street. He promptly blew his whistle and collected all available witnesses."

"All of whom," Gwen finished for her, "swore that it was Jep Jepson who hurried around the corner and into No. 27?"

"According to the newspapers, they did on the witness stand," Cherry said. "And an important witness for the prosecution, although a reluctant one, was the druggist, Palin. His evidence was completely inconclusive so far as I'm concerned, but it did help prove that Jep *could* have committed the crime."

"Why?" Josie demanded. "And how do you know he testified reluctantly?"

"Because," Cherry told her rather smugly, "I called him on the phone this afternoon from a public booth in the *News* building." She chuckled. "I'm afraid he somehow got the impression because I said I was calling from that building that I was a girl reporter. Anyway, the prosecuting attorney hammered at Mr. Palin in the same way that he hammered at Mrs. Herne. But unfortunately, while Mrs. Herne wasn't sure exactly when Jep went out for the aspirin, Mr. Palin *was* sure that he came into his store for it shortly after nine."

"How could he be so darn sure?" Gwen interrupted. "Does the man sit and watch the clock when he has nothing to do?"

"That's why I called him," Cherry explained. "His testimony wasn't published in the newspaper, but he told me he was sure of the time because when Jep came in he had just started mixing a prescription which takes a half hour from start to finish, an emulsion of cod-liver oil. The pharmacist was triturating when Jep bought the aspirin, and the prescription was ready to go when the cop blew his whistle at nine-thirty."

"Isn't that maddening?" Gwen exploded. "If only Mr. Palin had been mixing that emulsion of cod-liver oil for Dot who probably needed it more than the person who got it! Jep would of course have waited right there in the drugstore, and then he would have had an unbreakable alibi."

"It *is* maddening," Cherry agreed. "Jep insisted until the very end that after he bought the aspirin he hurried right back to Dot and Mrs. Herne and never left his flat again that night. So it couldn't have been he whom the patrolman and the bystanders saw hurry around the corner about twenty minutes later. However, the prosecuting attorney insisted that Jep did *not* go straight home, but lurked outside the drugstore until the coast was clear. He won the case when Mrs. Herne broke down and admitted that she couldn't be absolutely sure exactly how many minutes Jep was gone. Although, until confronted with Dot's innocent testimony, she was positive that Jep must have run both coming and going. He was out of breath when he came back with the aspirin. Palin verified this, but the prosecuting attorney twisted the words in his mouth so that in the end Palin seemed to be saying that Jep was panting and sweating with nervousness because he was on the verge of breaking into the pawnshop next door."

Gwen slid off the window seat and began pacing up and down the room. "I agree with you, Cherry," she said tautly. "If Jep had had the money to hire a good lawyer he would never have been convicted. Didn't his attorney cross-examine the witnesses at all?"

Cherry shook her head. "According to Mrs. Herne and Mr. Palin, he didn't. He must have handled the whole case in a halfhearted way, convinced from the beginning that his client was guilty." She stood up. "I'm not going to waste time criticizing Jep's lawyer. I'm going to go *see* him and confront him with a few facts he apparently overlooked."

Josie gasped. "You wouldn't dare, Cherry. He'd only laugh in your face. You're a nurse, remember, not a district attorney!"

"That's right," Gwen agreed soberly. "You haven't got any real facts, honey. All you can do is accuse the lawyer of negligence and you haven't even got any concrete proof of that."

Cherry, looking rather like the cat that swallowed the canary, smiled. "As a matter of fact, I *have* got concrete proof of his negligence, and when I've had a chat with Calahan I'll have more."

"Oh, my goodness," Josie groaned. "Are you going to

accuse the policeman, too, of helping to railroad Jep to jail?"

Cherry shook her head. "No, but I mean to find out exactly where the witnesses were when he saw someone hurrying around the corner that night. Those streets are usually poorly lighted, so unless they were awfully close to him, how could they all be sure that it was Jep they saw? Furthermore, how could they swear that whoever it was hurried into No. 27, not No. 25 or No. 29? You remember when we were visiting nurses how much one brownstone front looked like another?"

Josie nodded. "I was always going into the wrong entrance and would wade through all the names on the letter boxes before I realized my mistake."

"It's a perfectly natural mistake," Cherry added emphatically. "And one which I feel sure those bystanders made that fateful night. Figure it out for yourselves, girls. The hour was nine-thirty, and nobody suspected that a criminal was escaping with his loot right under their eyes. Not until *after* the cop blew his whistle. Whoever it was could have ducked into any one of those three similar buildings."

"How do you know they *are* similar?" Josie asked practically.

"That's just a guess," Cherry admitted. "I'll check to be sure when I see Calahan tomorrow. Mrs. Herne already told me they were owned by the same man, with one super in charge of the three. That usually means they were built at the same time with similar fronts."

"Okay," Josie said. "If Calahan proves you're right in your suspicions, you can certainly accuse Jep's lawyer of neglecting to cross-examine the State's witnesses. But what about that concrete proof you mentioned so slyly a while ago?"

Cherry thumbed through her notes. "Once Jep went to jail the hue and cry died down, and the last news report before his escape was so tiny I almost missed it. But if Mr. Brierson, Jep's lawyer, had been genuinely interested in the case he would have kept himself informed. Ah, here it is. I copied it down verbatim:

" 'Police say that all of the jewelry stolen in the West Avenue robbery has been recovered. It was obviously turned over to an accomplice who disposed of it in various pawnshops in different sections of the State. The only missing item is the gold watch, initialed H. T. A., and police said today that they do not expect to recover it. The distinctive monogram on the back would make it too hot for a fence to handle.' "

Josie laughed. "So that's your concrete evidence! If the police can't find that watch, Cherry Ames, what makes you think *you* can?"

"I not only can, but I will," Cherry said with more

conviction than she really felt then. "But that's not the point. The point is, Madam District Attorney, who was Jep's accomplice?"

"Don't ask me," Josie retorted. "You're the counsel for the defense."

"There wasn't any accomplice," Cherry said mysteriously. "But I can't be absolutely sure of that until after I've had a talk with Calahan."

Josie stared at her thoughtfully. "It sounds to me as though you're on the verge of stirring up a hornet's nest. Please take care, honey. Don't barge in where angels fear to tread."

Cherry was to remember that warning—when it was too late to heed it. But now she merely smiled sleepily. "Scram, girls, I've got to write some letters—to Mother and Charlie and Bertha and even a sarcastic thank-you note to that imp, Midge!"

She went back to her desk, but it was several minutes before she could rid her mind of the baffling mystery. What would she learn from Calahan and how would Mr. Brierson respond to her argument that he should reopen the case?

"Well, failing them," she decided, "I still have Mrs. Herne on my side. I know I can count on her help in proving Jep's innocence!"

CHAPTER VIII

Special Duty

ALTHOUGH CHERRY ENJOYED EVERY MINUTE OF HER work in Dr. Benham's clinic she thought the time would never come when she would be off duty. But at last it was four o'clock and she hurried to her room to change into street clothes.

"I suppose the best way to find out where Calahan lives," she decided, "is to ask at the precinct police station. That means taking a taxi. A cab driver would know in which precinct Duele Street is located."

In front of the hospital she discovered that the friendly doorman was not on duty, but Red's relief obligingly telephoned to the cab stand at the foot of the hill.

"They're sending one right up, miss," he said, tipping his cap.

A few minutes later Cherry was riding down the hill trying not to act as excited as she felt. "Please take me first to 27 Duele Street," she told the driver in what she hoped was a nonchalant voice. "But don't stop there. Just drive slowly past and then take me to the nearest police station."

The driver stopped for the light at the bottom of the hill and turned around to stare at her. "Now, what business would a pretty young lady like you have in that station?"

"I want to find out the home address of the policeman who patrols Duele Street in the evening," Cherry said meekly. "Will they give it to me, do you think?"

"Sure they will," the driver assured her. "But why you should want it, is beyond me."

Cherry laughed a little nervously. "The point is will *they* want to know why I want it?"

"Frankly, I don't think they'd be interested," he said, and realizing that she had no intention of satisfying his curiosity, he drove on in silence. As they passed by No. 27 Duele Street, Cherry saw to her satisfaction that the adjoining brownstone fronts were exactly alike.

"Well, that's that," she said. "Now to discover how much Calahan remembers about that fateful night."

Calahan, she learned from the genial sergeant behind the big desk at headquarters, lived just around the corner. "He'll likely be standing out in front smoking his after-breakfast cigar," he said with a grin. "He'll be in a good humor, too, after a long day's sleep. You can't miss him. A big fellow with hair as black and curly as yours and cheeks as red." The sergeant guffawed. "But not pretty, miss, like you. Calahan's a good man, but not even his mother would call him pretty."

Pretty is certainly not the word, Cherry decided with an inward giggle as she introduced herself to the big burly patrolman in front of his apartment house. He looked like a prize fighter, but he had the warmest and friendliest smile Cherry had ever seen.

"So you're one of the nurses at the hospital where they took Dot Jepson?" he asked, shaking her hand. "I'm glad to meet you. Any friend of Dot's is a friend of mine."

Cherry got right down to business then. "How about Dot's father, Calahan? Was he a good friend of yours too?"

"That he was," the policeman said heartily. "Why Jep stooped to petty larcency is something I'll never figure out."

"That's what I want to talk to you about," Cherry put in quickly. "Since knowing Dot, I've been thinking and reading a lot about that robbery. And I've come to the conclusion that it may well have been a case of mistaken identity. Are you, for instance, sure that it was Jep you saw hurrying away from the scene of the crime that night?"

Calahan stared at her in outraged amazement. "Me? Where did you ever get the idea that I testified against Jep? All that prosecuting attorney ever got out of me was that I saw *someone* sneaking around the corner just before my feet crunched on the broken glass from the pawnshop window."

"Well, then," Cherry said excitedly, "who *was* sure? Were any of the witnesses close enough to be absolutely positive that the man was Jep?"

Calahan scratched his head thoughtfully. "Now let me see. After I passed the pawnshop at nine, I turned off the Avenue and into Colvin Street, my regular route. I walked north, east, and south, and finally turned down Duele heading back toward the Avenue. About midway in the block, I caught up with the Blakes, an elderly couple, miss, on their way home after a game of cards with neighbors. They were walking too slowly for me, so I left them after a word or two and continued on to the Avenue. When I got there I saw someone hurry around the opposite corner, but didn't think anything of that then. Later when I blew my whistle, Palin came right out of his store and told me he thought, but he would never swear to it, that he had heard the crash of glass a few minutes before he heard my whistle. Then the Blakes came shuffling along and testified that they saw a man who looked like Jep dart inside No. 27 right after I left them."

"Oh, dear," Cherry moaned. "I wish they'd been as careful as Mr. Palin was and said they *thought* it was No. 27. Do you think they were near enough, Calahan, to be absolutely sure it wasn't one of the adjoining buildings?"

Calahan thought for a minute. "I couldn't say, miss, but they were as sure as I was, and as sorry to say it as I was, that the man answered Jep's description."

"All right," Cherry went on, reluctantly admiring the big policeman's cautiousness. "What is your theory about the accomplice?"

"Accomplice, miss?" Calahan frowned. "There wasn't any accomplice."

"There must have been," Cherry insisted. "No. 27 was searched from roof to cellar right after the robbery, and none of the stolen things were found. And yet, while Jep was still in prison, all of the jewelry turned up in other parts of the State. If Jep stole it, he must have handed it over to somebody else before he hurried home."

Calahan grinned at her. "If anybody else except Superman hurried away from the pawnshop that evening I would have seen him. The Avenue, as I told the judge, was deserted."

"It was deserted when you turned the corner about nine-thirty," Cherry pointed out. "But how about, say, nine-fifteen? Mr. Palin, remember, wasn't sure exactly when he heard the crash of glass."

Calahan's grin broadened. "Well, now, that's a funny thing, miss. It wasn't until after the Blakes said that the man they saw looked like Jep that Palin modified his statement. From then on Palin was never sure of anything except that Jep bought some aspirin in a hurry half an hour *before* I blew my whistle." He winked. "That gave Jep plenty of time to bring it back to his sick little girl, see?"

"I do see," Cherry said, "and it's a pity Jep's lawyer was so blind."

"He wasn't much good, and that's a fact," Calahan agreed. "But then Jep did have a motive. That you can't deny, miss."

Cherry sniffed. "I don't think he had any motive at all. And if his lawyer had any imagination he would have realized that from the very beginning."

Calahan shook his head sadly. "Frankly, miss, I think you've been misinformed on several points. I'd like to help you, but I think the best thing for you to do is talk it all over with Mr. Brierson. And if you'd be interested,

I have his phone number and address right here in my notebook."

Mr. Brierson, Cherry discovered an hour later, was as lacking in imagination as she had guessed he would be.

He was a pompous, middle-aged man who made no attempt to disguise the fact that he felt Cherry was wasting his valuable time.

"Get to the point, Miss Ames," he said brusquely. "I'm not interested in how dark the street was at that time of night. And my curiosity is only slightly aroused by your ridiculous statement that my client had no motive."

Cherry took a deep breath. "It's not a ridiculous statement, Mr. Brierson," she contradicted him. "Jep was temporarily out of work, I grant you, worried about his sick child, and down to his last cent. But the child did not become seriously ill until the night of the crime. He knew perfectly well then that he could receive free medical attention and nursing care for her by notifying Social Service. In fact, his neighbor, Mrs. Herne, told him when she sent him for the aspirin that she intended to call in the visiting nurse the next morning."

Mr. Brierson sighed with exasperation. "What, pray tell me, is pertinent in that rambling statement?"

"Just this," Cherry retorted. "Jep was not desperate.

His child would have been cared for while he got another job. And he could have got another job very easily. He was a skilled workman earning good pay before he quit in order to be with his daughter during the day. He was too proud to ask for outside help until he really needed it. It seems to me," she finished, "that a man who is too proud to beg is certainly too proud to steal."

The lawyer picked up a paperweight and slammed it back on his magohany desk. "My dear young woman," he snapped, "I have no doubt that you're an excellent nurse, but you would get nowhere in the legal profession. Have you proof that Jepson could have got employment in the near future?"

"Yes, I have," Cherry said, pretending to be meek. "Mrs. Herne, who has a great deal of influence with the owner of those three buildings on Duele Street, was arranging things so that Jep would get the superintendent's job. Besides a good salary, he would have had his rent free and could have kept an eye on Dot at the same time. The present super is on the verge of being fired. He is apparently no good at all."

"*Apparently*," the counselor sneered. "And I asked you for proof." He rose ponderously to his feet and held out his hand, a gesture of rude dismissal.

Cherry ignored it. "I'll get you proof when I find the

man who has in his possession a big gold watch with the initials H. T. A. on the back," she said quietly. "You know, of course, that everything else that was stolen turned up, shortly *after* Jep went to prison?"

Mr. Brierson cleared his throat. "I—er, didn't know. But his accomplice—"

Cherry laughed without humor. "It seems strange to me that the idea that Jep must have had an accomplice never entered the picture until after his conviction." She shrugged. "I suppose the answer is that everyone was in such a hurry to get him off to jail they just didn't think, not even you and the sympathetic judge. Everything happened so quickly I imagine No. 27 was still being exhaustively searched until the jewels began to show up in pawnshops in other parts of the state."

The lawyer blew out his cheeks. "Naturally. It would take a long time to do a thorough job on that tenement. Rotten floor boards, chinks in the plaster walls, the incinerator, the furnace, ash cans, garbage pails, etc., ad infinitum. Added to which, the tenants, sympathizing with Jepson, undoubtedly opposed the police every step of the way."

"Naturally," Cherry said, using the lawyer's own word and imitating his pompous tone of voice. "And quite rightly too, since the loot was undoubtedly hidden in one of the other adjoining buildings all the time." It was her turn to stand up. "And that's where the monogrammed watch is right now, Mr. Brierson, and it's in the possession of a tall, stoop-shouldered man who looks enough like Jepson to have been mistaken for him that night."

Mr. Brierson guffawed. "That is the most ridiculous statement you've made yet, Miss Ames. Even you must accept the fact that the—er—accomplice has destroyed that watch long ago."

"Not necessarily," Cherry said coolly. "The monogram was only mentioned in one tiny news write-up which I almost missed myself. And I'll bet the crook *did* miss it, as well as everyone else in the neighborhood. The police detectives probably kept it from the reporters during Jep's arrest and trial, hoping that the watch would eventually turn up somewhere in No. 27 and be the last bit of evidence against him."

Mr. Brierson swayed back on his heels with a sarcastic smile on his face. "And you don't think your petty thief has the sense to throw it into a furnace?"

"No, I don't," Cherry said airily. "Because he *is* petty. That crime was committed by a small-minded, lazy person who would rather risk a jail sentence than work for the money he needed—or wanted. That type of individual is a human magpie, robbing other people's nests instead of building one of his own. And a magpie, you know, Mr. Brierson, cannot resist anything that glitters. When he found he couldn't dispose of the watch through a fence, he decided to keep it in his pocket. And why not, since another man had already been sent to prison for the theft of it?"

The lawyer placed his finger tips on his desk top and stared down at them. "This magpie—this figment of your imagination—what makes you so sure that he lives in one of the adjoining buildings on Duele Street? My own personal theory is that the accomplice is a character Jepson met at the poolroom and lives in an entirely different neighborhood."

Cherry shook her head. "There was no accomplice, Mr. Brierson, and the real thief must live in the neighborhood. He was familiar with Calahan's beat for one thing, and, for another, he knew that the pawnshop is the old-fashioned type, no iron grating across the window, no automatic burglar alarms. Furthermore, as I tried to explain to you when I first arrived, the witnesses at that time of night—"

Mr. Brierson's crisp secretary came in then, so Cherry knew that he must have pressed a button on his desk, signaling he wished the interview ended. Without waiting for the secretary's excuse, Cherry tossed her head and left. There was no point in discussing the matter further with a man who was obviously still so convinced of Jep's guilt.

The Jepson case, she realized, was closed so far as the lawyer and police were concerned. Both the thief and his accomplice were still at large, but such petty thieves would surely be picked up sooner or later on some other charge.

And now Cherry began to worry for fear Jep *would* be arrested before she could solve the mystery.

"Oh, dear," she moaned inwardly, "I've got to find that other tall, stoop-shouldered man right away. I'll go to see Mrs. Herne tomorrow the minute I get off duty. She'll know which one of her neighbors fits that description."

But Cherry, in spite of her plans, did not get a chance to visit Mrs. Herne until the following week, the last week in October. The morning after she had discussed her latest clues with Gwen and Josie, she awoke early, full of anticipation.

Reporting for duty half an hour ahead of time, she was arranging the day's charts when she suddenly had the uncomfortable feeling that someone was watching her. She whirled around to find Dr. Laughton sitting placidly at the desk.

"My goodness," she gasped. "Did you drop from the ceiling, sir?"

His eyes twinkled, but he said tartly, "No, I simply walked in through the door. Did I startle you?"

Cherry laughed. "Well, you don't exactly stamp your feet or clear your throat or slam doors, do you?"

He shook his head soberly. "No. Should I? Of course

not. This is a hospital, not a football stadium. People who work in a hospital are usually so busy and so absorbed by their work, I'm confident an Indian in full regalia could stroll down the corridor without getting so much as a passing glance." He chuckled. "If I were a fugitive from justice I would seek refuge in a hospital, and feel perfectly safe."

Cherry flushed guiltily. Had the Chief's bright blue eyes been reading her mind? Then at his next remark her sense of guilt deepened and her cheeks flamed.

"I'm disappointed in you, girl," he said abruptly.

Cherry stared at him wordlessly. What had she done? Had her interest in the Jepson case been making her neglectful of her work? No, yesterday when the clinic closed, Dr. Benham had praised her handling of the children.

The Chief was leaning forward to add sternly, "I asked you, Cherry Ames, to get acquainted with my staff and hospital. Instead of which, you leave the grounds the minute you are off duty."

"I'm sorry, sir," Cherry said, hoping her cheeks were not as red as they felt. "I—"

He held up his hand. "No excuses. But I must repeat, I am disappointed, in both you *and* Davie Lane."

"Disappointed in *him?*" Cherry gasped. "But why, sir?"

"He spends all his time off duty going to parties."

"How do you know that?" Cherry demanded.

He shrugged. "What else can I assume? He doesn't hang around here, and as often as not drives off with my flibbertigibbet granddaughter. I suppose meeting the influential people Leonie introduces him to makes him a good politician, but it does not convince me that he is worthy of the Residency."

"He *does* deserve the appointment, sir," Cherry contradicted him, not meaning to be impudent. "Everyone around here has somehow got the wrong impression of David Lane. He's not a backslapper. He's a very able and serious young man. Of course he wants to get to the top, and he will, but in the meantime he wants to get all the training he can. He thinks of the Residency as a vitally important rung on his ladder, not as a rich political plum."

Dr. Laughton smiled briefly. "Then why does he drive off every afternoon with my empty-headed granddaughter?"

Cherry bit her lip. "Perhaps she merely drives him into the center of town, sir. An assistant resident can't afford many taxis. And I happen to know that David is working nights with a newspaper writer on a series of medical articles. He's as much of a crusader on the subject of acquainting the public with the symptoms and cure of diabetes as Dr. Benham is on the subject of deafness. In fact," she finished breathlessly, "David Lane is interested in the whole field of medicine!"

The Chief's eyebrows shot up quizzically. "And what makes you think he deserves the appointment more than Alan Dodd does? If you had complied with my request you might have become sufficiently acquainted with that young man for your opinion to have some value. But as it is—"

"You're perfectly right, sir," Cherry interrupted, ashamed of her unfair but well-meant recommendation of David. "I've never worked with Alan Dodd, so I have no business deciding against him. My opinion was based on the fact that most of the staff apparently thinks that David is the better physician of the two."

He glanced at her shrewdly. "Would you like to work with Al, Cherry?"

She nodded enthusiastically.

"Well, that can easily be arranged." He rubbed his small, immaculate hands together happily. "Our busiest hours on the wards are from four to eight. The place is cluttered up with visitors just before the children have to be fed and prepared for the night, and at that same time we're shorthanded because the nurses leave in two shifts to go to dinner. Now, my plan is that you might offer to help us out during those hours by accompanying

Dr. Dodd on his evenings rounds, taking the place of the head nurse on each floor. Will you do it, Cherry?"

"I'd love to," Cherry said promptly, thinking that this would give her invaluable experience toward her goal of becoming a night supervisor sometime. "But, not being familiar with any of the cases, would I be much help?"

"You can read and write, can't you?" he demanded tartly. Then as Cherry's nervousness showed on her face, he added more gently:

"Our supervisor, Mrs. Welch, can't possibly have at her finger tips the details of every case, child, and yet she is in full charge of the entire hospital at night. What do you think we have charts for, Cherry Ames?" he went on.

"No one's going to expect you to step into Mrs. Welch's shoes overnight, girl. Well, will you help us out?"

"Of course," Cherry said.

And not until later did she realize that this extra duty meant she would not be able to visit Mrs. Herne for another week. By the time she got back to the Nurses' Residence and changed into street clothes, it would be too late to start for 27 Duele Street.

When Alan Dodd heard of the arrangement, he made no effort to disguise his delight.

"What a break," he said with an admiring grin at Cherry. "And will Dave ever be burned up! I've been trying to talk him into a swap ever since you arrived so I could work with Dr. Benham, but he would have none of it! Now he'll be sorry."

Cherry laughed. "Wait till you see how I work out. Maybe *you'll* be sorry."

The week passed quickly, and, although Cherry was too exhausted most of the time to think about the mystery, it was worth it, because she enjoyed every minute of her work with both the young residents.

Alan, she soon decided, was a born pediatrician and she was sure he would have no trouble at all building up a lucrative practice whenever he felt he was ready. He was also a very pleasant young man to work with and frequently consulted her opinion before writing an order on a small patient's chart.

"This is a good opportunity for you to get some practice," he said when she shyly told him of her secret ambition. "Now, in this case would you prescribe aspirin, sulpha, or penicillin?"

At another time he said, "You're alone on the floor. What would you do, Cherry?"

"I'd have you dragged out of bed at once," she said without hesitation.

"Right." He nodded approvingly. "In a case like this,

no nurse should take the full responsibility. When you've learned when to take it, and when *not* to, you'll have arrived."

Soon all of Alan's little patients were calling her Cherry, and she was greeted warmly every evening by the head nurse on each floor. "Wish this weren't just temporary duty, Miss Ames," they would say. "We could use someone like you around here permanently."

Even busy Mrs. Welch, who came on duty at seven, stopped long enough once to praise her briskly. "It's a pleasure to tour the wards after you and Dr. Dodd have made your rounds, Miss Ames," she said, and hurried away.

During this extra duty, Cherry met up with several of the friends she had made while in training. She passed Mom several times in the corridors, and, to the delight of Alan Dodd, was hugged and kissed with no respect given her crisply starched uniform. Old Lucy, she discovered with pleasure, was one of the maids on Surgical.

Whenever they met on the wards or in the elevators, Cherry would glance suspiciously at the wagon Lucy was wheeling and ask, "Any rabbits in those compartments this evening?" And Lucy would go off into gales of laughter.

Cherry saw Dot every evening at bedtime too, and

never missed a chance for a quick look at the "Frog Prince," wondering what there could be in the painting to remind Dot of her father: a tall, thin man, slightly stoop-shouldered, with premature gray hair.

One evening, as Alan Dodd was soberly examining the child's teddy bear in obedience to her command, Dot said to Cherry:

"I'm mad at Dave. He never comes to see me any more."

"That's because he's not on night duty now, honey," Alan explained, looping his stethoscope around his neck.

"And during the day," Cherry went on, "he works downstairs in the clinic."

Dot nodded. "I'm going to be able to go downstairs all by myself pretty soon," she said. "And then I'll see my daddy and Dave and everybody whenever I want to."

"Oh," Cherry said softly. "Then your daddy works downstairs too?"

"Well, not 'zactly." The little girl avoided Cherry's eyes. "I'm not s'posed to talk about that. It's a secret."

Outside in the corridor Alan gave Cherry an amused look. "Surely you don't believe the kid when she rambles on about seeing her father?"

Cherry laughed and quickly changed the subject. "One thing I'd like to know, Alan," she said, "is why the student nurses apparently get so upset when they work with David and perform so beautifully for you."

He stared at her incredulously. "What ever gave you that impression? Quite the opposite is the truth. Dave keeps them on their toes; they wouldn't dare not be alert when he's on the floor. But I'm so easygoing the backward gals fall into a stupor. Naturally they don't make any glaring mistakes, but neither do they perform brilliantly." He chuckled. "I'd say they learn about twice as much twice as fast working with Dave."

"Tell me the truth, Alan," Cherry suddenly blurted. "Do you want to be the new Resident?"

"Frankly, no," he said promptly. "I want to go into private practice. Besides, Dave's the man for the job."

When she reported to Dr. Laughton at the end of the week, Cherry had an opportunity to repeat this conversation to him. But she was disappointed, for he seemed completely unimpressed by the fact that Alan did not really want the appointment.

"Well, well," he said noncommittally, "there are several up-and-coming young pediatricians over at City Hospital. One or two of them have been highly recommended by the trustees."

Before Cherry could say anything more he changed the subject. "By the way, Cherry, did you notify Social Service that the home life of that Fowler boy should be investigated?"

Cherry gulped. "Oh, my goodness, I forgot all about it. I've never even thought about Rudie Fowler since that morning. I'll ask Josie Franklin what became of him. She'll know—he was in her clinic."

He shook his head. "I'm afraid she won't know any more than I do. He didn't wait for his turn that day and, according to the records which I just inspected, he's never been back. The visiting nurse reported that the child's father claims his condition is improved and he no longer needs medical attention. I was just wondering, that's all. He looked like a sick youngster to me."

"He did to me too," Cherry agreed. "And I should have dropped a hint to the social worker."

"You've been pretty busy, my dear." He smiled. "I'll take care of the matter myself."

When he had gone, Cherry stared after him, thinking, "That boy *was* sick, and I'll bet he *does* need medical attention. He probably ran away because he was afraid the cure might be worse than the disease. And as for his father telling the visiting nurse that Rudie's condition has improved—well, I just don't believe it!"

And then, remembering that today when she got off duty she could at last pay a visit to Mrs. Herne, Cherry dismissed the Fowler boy from her mind.

CHAPTER IX

Rudie Fowler's Story

IT WAS AFTER FOUR-THIRTY WHEN CHERRY FINISHED filing her charts, and she was hurrying out of the ENT clinic when the phone rang. Both of the doctors had already gone so Cherry answered it and Gwen's voice said:

"You don't have to take that long trek out to Duele Street, Cherry. Mrs. Herne is here. She says she'll meet you down in the waiting room in half an hour."

"Wonderful," Cherry cried. "I've got plenty of work to keep me busy until then."

Thirty minutes later she and Mrs. Herne were seated cozily together on the black leather settee. Cherry didn't wait a second getting down to the root of the matter.

"Mrs. Herne," she began, "is there anybody in your neighborhood who looks enough like Jep Jepson to have been mistaken for him that night? I mean, a tall, thin, slightly stoop-shouldered man with perhaps very blond hair instead of prematurely gray."

Mrs. Herne started. "Why, you must be talkin' about our lazy, good-for-nothin' super, Miss Cherry. He's ash blond, he is, and tall and thin, and he slouches along not because he's overworked but because he's too lazy to hold his head up."

Cherry could hardly control her excitement. "And he lives on the premises rent free, doesn't he?"

"That's right," Mrs. Herne told her. "In No. 29. He and his little boy, Rudie, although why the owner doesn't fire that loafer, Fowler, I'll never know."

It was Cherry's turn to start. "Rudie . . . Fowler? . . . Are you talking about Rudie Fowler's father?"

"And who else would I be talkin' about?" Mrs. Herne demanded. "I was tellin' you about him the other day. It was him I told the owner he should fire and hire Jep in his place. A fine super, Jep would have been, too, and Fowler won't last much longer. No heat, no hot water, the halls so cluttered and the light bulbs so cobwebby, a body hardly dares to walk along 'em at night. Now, before that man drove her into runnin' away, Mrs. Fowler used to keep things tidy, workin' nights and weekends, and she with a job cookin' all day in that restaurant."

"Oh," Cherry gasped. "Did Rudie's mother run away?"

"Well, yes and no," Mrs. Herne said evasively. "I only know she didn't come home one evenin' after work, a payday it was, and I don't blame her. She never complained but we all knew he took her pay envelope away from her the minute she put her foot in that dark basement apartment. I've heard him myself shoutin' at her, 'Give me that money, Lily. Give it to me or I'll break your wrist.' And her pleadin' with him, 'Leave me just a little, Rudolph. The boy needs a warm sweater.'"

Cherry clenched her fists. "He must be a terrible, terrible man. No wonder Mrs. Fowler ran away—but why didn't she take Rudie with her?"

Mrs. Herne snorted. "How could she? She'd have to go home and get him and then that Fowler would have taken all her money. You can't travel on air, Miss Cherry, and you can't eat it either. Speakin' of which, the boy's been half-starved ever since. I don't think that Fowler keeps a speck of food in the house. Eats out himself and spends the rest of the time hangin' around pool-rooms."

Cherry remembered how thin Rudie had looked that day and how surprised she was that he had so much strength. "His father must give him something to eat," she said. "He wouldn't dare let the boy starve to death."

Mrs. Herne shrugged. "You'd believe me if you'd set the platters of food in front of him that I have. He eats as though he couldn't get enough, and always thirsty too. 'Could I have some orange juice, Mrs. Herne? Got any of that cider left?' At least that's the way it was until a week or so ago, and I must say I'm glad he's stopped comin' around. A nice lad, Rudie was, until his mother left. Seems as though that did somethin' to him. Acts tough now, imitatin' his father, and no manners, never a 'please' or a 'thank you,' and always snatchin' and pushin' and shovin'. I did the best I could for him, for his mother's sake, the poor little frightened woman, and now the boy's sick and I don't know where to write her to tell her so. She'd come back, if she knew, as afraid as she is of Fowler, and stay long enough, anyway, to nurse him back to health."

Cherry sighed, wishing more than ever now that she had reported her suspicions to the social worker that first day. "How sick is Rudie?" she asked.

"That I don't know," Mrs. Herne told her. "I didn't even know he'd taken to his bed until this mornin' when I passed Miss Gardner, our visitin' nurse, on the street. 'Mrs. Herne,' she says to me, 'that Fowler boy is no better, worse if anything since the day I sent him to the clinic and he refused to be examined.'

"I says to her, 'I knew nothin' of that, Miss Gardner.

I haven't seen him lately, but I figured somebody else has been feedin' him. Are you tellin' me he's sick in bed with no one to care for him and you so overworked you should be in bed yourself?'

"She smiles and says, 'I am busy, Mrs. Herne, so busy I didn't have a chance to check up on Rudie until just now. And would you believe it, his father tried to keep me out of the basement. Claims the boy's just lazy, that's why he hasn't gone to school. But he's sick, Mrs. Herne, I'm sure of it, although his father wouldn't let me do much more than peek at him. Rudie was half-asleep, but I could see, even in that dark, damp room, that he's lost a lot more weight.'

" 'Of course he's sick,' I says. 'Rudie Fowler can't sit still a minute let alone take to his bed in the daytime.'

" 'Well, then, Mrs. Herne,' she says, 'will you do me a favor? Look in on him this evening. His father might let *you* take his temperature.'

" 'I'd be glad to, Miss Gardner,' I says. 'His father will likely be out playing pool around nine, but even if he isn't, I'll put a thermometer in that child's mouth if I have to call in Calahan to hold Fowler while I do it.' "

"Good for you." Cherry smiled. "And let me know how you think he is too, won't you? I feel sort of responsible. I met him the day he came to the clinic but didn't stay, and then I forgot all about him."

"You don't feel half as responsible as I do," Mrs. Herne said. "When Lily Fowler ran away she sent me a message asking me to look out for him. She also said she'd—" Mrs. Herne stopped, her freckled face flushed. "Never mind about that. She's got her reasons, I guess, poor little thing. And that Fowler fillin' the boy full of lies, sayin' his mother deserted him because she got sick of spendin' all the money she earned on food and clothes for him instead of buyin' pretty things for herself. If you ask me, she's saving every cent so that someday she can send for the boy."

"Of course she is," Cherry said gently. She could understand now why Rudie, influenced by his father, had shouted defiantly, "I hate my father, but I hate my mother worse. That's why I tear up her letters."

"Something has got to be done about Fowler," she told Mrs. Herne, and then all at once she knew what *could* be done. He could be sent to jail, not for mistreating his wife and child, but—*for the pawnshop robbery!* The description of the man who hurried around the corner that night fit Fowler as well as it did Jep, and Fowler had a motive. Missing the money he took from his wife every payday, he may well have been tempted by the display in the show window, and gradually planned the robbery. And it was sheer luck that Jep, buying aspirin for his little girl, had been in the vicinity of the pawnshop that night. Otherwise, the by-standers might have accused Fowler of the crime, or at least, they might not have been so sure that the man they saw had *white* hair.

"Something certainly should be done about that man," Mrs. Herne was saying. "And I for one—"

"Where was *he* the night of the robbery?" Cherry interrupted. "Does anybody know?"

Mrs. Herne looked startled. "Oh, Miss Cherry! Then you think—oh, my goodness, of course that's who it was Calahan and the others saw." Then her face fell. "But it won't work, honey. It was a good idea, but Fowler had an alibi. I thought for a minute we might find someone who would remember he was in that poolroom across the street from the drugstore around nine that night, 'cause that's where he is when he isn't eatin' and sleepin'. He could have watched the whole block from the poolroom window just as easy without anyone suspectin' anything."

"Alibi?" Cherry repeated. "You said he had an alibi, but I don't understand. Was Fowler ever questioned as a possible suspect?"

"Oh, no, Miss Cherry," Mrs. Herne said. "But everyone in the neighborhood who might have seen somethin' was questioned that night and the followin' mornin'. Most of us, except Fowler and Rudie, came out on the street soon as Calahan blew his whistle. And I was down in the basement of No. 29 the next mornin', complainin' about no hot water, when Calahan came in. He wanted to know if Fowler, being the super, might have been in our buildin' around nine-thirty, and if so, had he seen anyone hurry up the stairs. But Fowler said he hadn't seen anythin' or anyone, 'cause he'd fallen asleep after dinner and didn't wake up till I woke him, hammerin' on the door. Then up pipes Rudie and says he knows his father was asleep when the robbery was committed cause Rudie was listenin' to his favorite radio program which starts at nine and keeps goin' till ten. He says to the cop, 'I had it tuned up real loud, Mr. Calahan, and my pop was so sound asleep he didn't ever holler at me. Guess that's why we didn't hear your whistle last night.' "

"A very neat little alibi," Cherry said suspiciously. "And I'll bet Fowler was the only one on the whole block who could prove exactly where he was between nine and nine-thirty. You couldn't, remember, because you didn't bother to look at the clock when you sent Jep out for the aspirin? An innocent person doesn't necessarily remember where he was every minute of the day or night, but a crook is generally smart enough to provide himself with an alibi *before* he commits the crime."

"Oh, oh." Mrs. Fowler began to rock back and forth, groaning. "You've figured it all out, Miss Cherry, but too late. Now that I think of it, Rudie looked as though he'd been cryin', and he spoke his piece to Calahan like a little parrot, instead of naturallike, all mixed up, the way a boy'd talk, in a hurry to put in his two cents' worth."

Cherry nodded understandingly. "But it's not too late, Mrs. Herne. I'll go see Rudie Fowler myself and if he's well enough make him confess that he lied to Calahan that morning."

Mrs. Fowler shook her head, and the rusty feathers on her outmoded hat flapped dismally. "He'd never do it, Miss Cherry, but not because he's too sick to talk. Rudie's so scared of his father he hardly dares breathe when he's around."

"I don't intend to question Rudie when his father's around," Cherry said. "And I'll get a confession out of him without his knowing it. I'll get him to talking about his favorite radio program, and then when he's off his guard I'll ask him if he remembers what the show was like the night of the robbery. I know kids, Mrs. Herne. If Rudie lied to Calahan, it'll show on his face."

"That it will," Mrs. Herne agreed. "But how will you get to see the boy? Fowler'll never let you on the premises."

Cherry refused to be crushed. "I'll go sometime when he isn't on the premises himself."

"That won't do you any good," Mrs. Herne told her. "The door to the basement is always locked. Orders of the owner, and Fowler's the only one who has the keys."

"But that's ridiculous," Cherry objected. "How does Rudie get in and out when his father's away?"

"He doesn't," Mrs. Herne told her flatly. "He's always either locked in or locked out, the poor little creature. No wonder he's got the bad reputation of hangin' around the streets nights. He's slept half the night at my place more than once."

"How dreadful," Cherry cried. "But all that's going to be stopped," she added, remembering that the great Dr. Laughton was going to investigate the case. But would he have the time to go there himself? Of course not. He would simply notify the understaffed Social Service. It might be days before anyone got around to calling at No. 29 Duele Street since this was not, apparently, an emergency case.

Or was it? The child was sick and probably alone, locked in a dark, damp basement room. And then Cherry was struck with an idea and she jumped up excitedly. "But you're going there tonight, Mrs. Herne. How do *you* expect to get in?"

Mrs. Herne stared at her. "Why, I never thought

about that. But what I'll do of course is, if Fowler's out, send my Jerry around to that poolroom and get the key. Fowler'll give it to him, Miss Cherry, never fear. Jerry's a big man with a quick temper, although as gentle as a lamb with children, lovin' them all as he does."

"Well, then," Cherry said triumphantly, "we have nothing to worry about. I'll get a confession out of Rudie Fowler this very night, Mrs. Herne. Because *I'm* going to look in on him at nine, instead of you!"

CHAPTER X

A Daring Plan

THE FRECKLES STOOD OUT IN THE WHITENESS OF MRS. Herne's plump face. "You'll do nothing of the sort, Cherry Ames," she said, as though she were addressing a naughty little girl. "Imagine a nice young lady like you payin' visits in our neighborhood at that time of night!"

Cherry laughed. "Not so long ago I worked in a district like yours, Mrs. Herne, as a visiting nurse, and I loved it and everybody in it."

"That's different," Mrs. Herne said emphatically. "Even a rough man respects a nurse's uniform. That pretty blue suit of Miss Gardner's gets her into places where even I wouldn't care to go after dark. It's a perfectly respectable neighborhood in the daytime, Miss Cherry, but at night tough men from other districts come and hang around that poolroom. I wouldn't want you even passin' one of 'em on the street."

"I'm not the least bit afraid," Cherry said. "But if it'll make you feel any better, I'll wear my own visiting nurse's uniform. It's hanging in my closet at the Nurses' Residence right now, and on the shelf above it is my hat to match."

"Well, that does make me feel better." Mrs. Herne sighed. "Yes, you'd best wear your uniform, Miss Cherry. Otherwise, Fowler might be home at nine and he'd never let you in without it." She frowned worriedly. "But he might not even let you in at that, uniform or no uniform. He was very rude to Miss Gardner only this mornin', slammin' the door in her face and tellin' her not to be comin' back and botherin' him." She snorted. "Said he could take care of the boy himself, and he not even knowin' which end of a thermometer is up. And you can't force you way in, Miss Cherry. There's some law that says you can't."

"I don't want to force my way in," Cherry said. "Oh, dear. Is there any way we can be sure Fowler will be away at nine?"

Mrs. Herne thought for a minute. "I tell you what, Miss Cherry, we're doin' a lot of unnecessary worryin'. Fowler doesn't even know you're on earth, so why should he change his habits this one night? He'll be in that poolroom at nine, don't you fret, and I'll have the key waitin' for you if you'll drop into my place first."

She heaved herself to her feet and Cherry hugged her impulsively. "You're an angel, Mrs. Herne. No wonder everyone loves you!"

Mrs. Herne patted her big hat back in place, her plump face beaming. "Now don't you be so sure that everybody loves me. Fowler, for one, doesn't, although he's afraid of me, on account of me and the owner bein' such good friends. Fowler doesn't love anyone, Miss Cherry, and don't you be forgettin' that. If he should come back while you're there with Rudie, you just get up and go quietly. He might act ugly. In fact, I'm warnin' you, he *would* act ugly if you didn't do just what he said."

"I'll be careful," Cherry promised meekly. She said good-bye to Mrs. Herne in the rotunda and hurried down the steps to the tunnel. She had just time to wash up before first dinner which she wanted to have with Gwen who would be on night duty tonight in the regular nurse's place. And by this time tomorrow, Halloween, they would all be in Hilton!

Cherry tingled all over in anticipation of a weekend at home, but right now she could hardly wait to discuss with Gwen her plan of visiting Rudie Fowler. Cherry was sure she could make the boy betray the fact that he had lied to Calahan the morning after the robbery. And she also hoped that she might find out from Rudie whether or not his father had a big gold watch. Finding that out was even more important than breaking down Fowler's so-called alibi. And Gwen, Cherry knew, would be as excited about the whole venture as she was. But Josie, she felt sure, would be hard to convince.

During dinner Gwen listened attentively as Cherry outlined her scheme. She frowned every now and then, but in the end, she said enthusiastically:

"You're a bright gal, Ames, and a brave one. I'm not sure I'd risk bearding that Fowler in his den, alone. But more power to you! My only objection is that I can't go along." She laughed. "I wouldn't be much good, but at least I can scream in an emergency."

Cherry grinned. "Nobody's going to have to scream, Gwen. Even if Fowler should come home while I'm there, he won't be suspicious because I'll be wearing my V.N. uniform."

Gwen's eyebrows shot up. "You'll be wearing *what*?"

Cherry stared at her. "I thought I told you. I brought along my suit and hat and I'm going to wear them to-night. If anybody should ask any questions, I'm simply Miss Gardner's relief nurse."

"Oh, *oh, OH!*" Gwen groaned. "Where are your good resolutions, Cherry?"

Cherry's face fell. "I never thought about that, Gwen," she mumbled. "I have no business wearing that uniform without an assignment from the Visiting Nurse Service, have I?"

Gwen didn't bother to answer the rhetorical question. Instead she said thoughtfully, "You've got to wear it for your own safety. Just be careful, honey. And whatever you do, don't let your enthusiasm carry you up to my floor when you come back. Not until after you've changed. You might run into the Night Supervisor, Mrs. Welch, and heaven have mercy on your career if she catches you in that outfit."

Cherry giggled, a little nervously. "I'll be careful not to run into anybody like that, Gwen," she said.

"Knowing you," Gwen said dubiously, "I'm not so sure of that. But one thing is certain. Tired as I am, there's not a chance in the world of my falling asleep on duty tonight. I'll be worrying about you every minute."

Later, back in her room at Crowley, Cherry surveyed herself in the mirror. She had brushed her black curls until they fairly danced, up and around the brim of her navy felt hat. There was not a wrinkle in her tailored jacket and skirt, and she had washed and ironed the white broadcloth blouse.

"You look brisk enough to impress even Fowler," she

told herself. "But let's hope the opportunity never arises."

Then she heard the door open behind her and saw in the mirror that Josie was standing there, her mouth open in amazement.

Cherry wheeled around guiltily. "Hello, Franklin," she said with more airiness than she felt. "How was second dinner?"

Josie ignored the question. "Cherry Ames," she said slowly, "what are you up to now?"

Cherry took off her hat and whirled it on one finger. "As a matter of fact," she said, "I think I'd be safer if I carry this. And," reaching into her closet, "with my rain-coat over the uniform nobody on the Spencer grounds will even guess I'm wearing a visiting nurse's uniform."

Josie sank down on the bed. "You're not going to do it, Cherry," she said. "I didn't believe it when Gwen told me just now. You *can't*. You'll be caught sure as anything."

Cherry's knees felt weak. What had Dr. Joe said about Dr. Laughton? "No pranks, Cherry. Van wouldn't hesitate to dismiss you if you let your impulsiveness lead you into a violation of the rules and regulations." And before that he had cautioned her:

"He pretends to be as meek as Moses, but don't let him fool you."

Cherry thought about the tunnel between Crowley and Children's. En route to the hospital would the Chief suddenly appear from nowhere? She shuddered. His bright eyes could probably see right through a brown raincoat and the paper bag in which she was now tucking her hat. Then what would happen?

"Then," Cherry told herself, "I'd make him see I'm not really doing anything wrong. If he knew the circumstances, he'd understand how important it is that I see Rudie Fowler tonight—for Rudie's sake as well as Dot's—and eventually, her father's."

Aloud she said to Josie, "That boy may be really very sick. I'm a nurse. What I wear when I go to see him isn't important."

"Yes, it is important," Josie corrected her. "The reason you're wearing that uniform is that you don't dare go where you're going without it." She suddenly jumped up and put her arms around Cherry. "Oh, honey, don't go. Please don't. You may not get caught before you leave the grounds, but something much worse might happen to you at the other end."

Cherry hugged her. "Don't worry about me, Josie. I'll be all right. I'm not the least bit afraid of anything." Then she pulled herself free and darted out of the room.

But she *was* afraid—afraid of being caught by Dr.

Van Laughton—and she held her breath as she scurried through the tunnel. At the top of the stairs on the other side, she let it out slowly. Now for a dash across the rotunda and outside to the doorman's telephone booth just beyond the entrance. She'd stay with him in the shadows there until he put her into a cab, and then she'd be safe!

Cherry started across the rotunda feeling as though the hospital were one big eye, watching her suspiciously. Half of her wanted to run and the other half warned her that was the surest way of attracting attention. She had almost reached the door when a voice called out, "Hi, Cherry," and her heart stopped beating for a second.

Her whole body was frozen with fright, but at last she forced herself to turn around. It was Alan Dodd, and he was grinning so broadly that Cherry almost sighed out loud with relief. Alan was obviously so happy about something he wouldn't, to paraphrase the Chief, have noticed if she were wearing the full regalia of an Indian.

"Both Dave and I can come to your house party to-morrow, Cherry," he said delightedly. "I've just been talking to the Resident, and he seemed to think he could stagger through the weekend without us. I convinced him that there are a couple of interns who almost make sense sometimes. Those two are going to step into Dave's and my shoes pretty soon, anyway, so I thought they might get in a little practice ahead of time."

"Wonderful," Cherry cried. "And did you really mean it when you said you'd drive all of us to Hilton in your car?"

"Sure. It's not very handsome, but it'll hold the five of us easily." He flexed his hands tiredly. "Well, here I go for my last stretch of night duty for a long, long time. It'll be Dave's turn when we get back on Sunday." He hurried away toward the elevators, and Cherry slipped quickly through the door. Halfway down the steps she stopped and clapped her hand over her mouth to keep from crying out.

Silhouetted against the glass of the doorman's phone booth was a tall, thin, slightly stoop-shouldered man! He was hatless, and, in the dim light of the interior, he looked to Cherry as though he *might* have blond, or even gray hair. She stood watching him in amazement as he finished telephoning, and unfolded the door.

The light inside the booth automatically went out and as the man emerged into the brightly lighted area near the steps he clapped his cap back on his head.

It was Red, the friendly doorman, walking erect now, as though proud of his uniform. Cherry stared at the spindle-shaped brass buttons that marched down the front of his coat. And then she noticed for the first time that they were held in place by ornamental gold loops of braid.

Those, of course, were Dot's "frogs." And the man who was smiling pleasantly up at Cherry must be Jepson, his only disguise, dyed hair and an erect carriage!

CHAPTER XI

At No. 29

CHERRY THOUGHT FAST. SHOULD SHE TELL JEP JEPSON now that she knew who he was, or should she wait until after collecting more evidence toward proving his innocence?

The prudent thing, she knew, would be to wait. But Cherry was anything but prudent. Furthermore, Jep, the innocent victim, might provide her with additional information about Fowler which might in turn lead to more clues when she visited No. 29.

She started determinedly down the steps. "Good evening, Red. Remember me, Cherry Ames?"

He tipped his cap. "Indeed, I do, miss. How could I forget such a pretty face?"

"I see you're on the four to midnight shift now," she

said conversationally. "I should think you'd get awfully tired and lonely standing out here for eight hours at a stretch."

"Well, no, miss," he said. "Not lonely—always plenty of people coming in and out. And not tired either. I have time off for a bite of supper at six, and then a sandwich and a cup of coffee at ten when one of the engineers relieves me. Do you want me to telephone down to the stand and have a cab sent up for you?"

Cherry nodded. "Please." She followed him across the driveway to the booth. When he came out he said:

"It'll take about ten minutes, miss. You'll no doubt want to wait inside. I'll let you know when the cab arrives, and you can be sure I won't let anyone else take it."

"Thank you, Red."

Cherry reached into her handbag for a tip. Something crackled and she realized that it was Dot's torn letter which she had finally mended. At the last minute, before donning her uniform, she had decided to take it with her, planning to read it to Rudie in the hope that she could convince him that parents *do* write nice letters. It seemed so tragic for Mrs. Fowler to write to her son, not knowing that he tore up the envelopes before opening them.

And now, feeling the taped pages between her fingers, Cherry decided to use the letter for another purpose. She pulled it out and handed it to the doorman.

"I've read this, Jep," she said softly. "It's a beautiful letter. We all love your Mouse—almost as much as you do."

He drew back and for a moment Cherry thought he might turn and run. She reached out quickly and touched one of the gold frogs on his coat. "You don't have to be afraid of me, Jep. I've thought you were innocent since the day Dot told me you were her Frog Prince."

His big shoulders slumped. "I shouldn't have talked to her like that. I shouldn't have risked going to see her. But I couldn't help it, miss. I couldn't stand thinking about it any longer—her being here sick and so far away from me. That's why I broke out of jail. But I won't run away now. You call the cops and I'll go with them as meek as a lamb."

"I have no intention of calling the police, Jep," Cherry said firmly. "I know you didn't rob that pawnshop, and I'm on my way now to proving it."

He stared at her incredulously. "You don't know what you're saying, Miss Cherry. I couldn't even make my own lawyer believe me when I told him I didn't steal those things."

"He didn't know then what I found out last week," Cherry said. "You couldn't have stolen those things and hidden them somewhere in your apartment house, because they all, except the watch, turned up in other parts of the state *after* you went to jail. When I find who still has the watch, I'll have found the real thief. That's why I'm going to see Rudie Fowler tonight. I suspect strongly that his father has a big gold watch with the initials H. T. A. on the back."

"Fowler?" Jep's pleasant face was twisted momentarily with rage. "You think he's the thief?"

"I do," Cherry said, and told him why. When she had finished he said:

"But you mustn't go there alone, Miss Cherry. He's a dangerous man, he is. Treated his wife so cruelly she ran away, poor little thing. I'll never forget that night. It was she who helped me get the night watchman job in the same building where she worked. I'd just signed in my first day on duty when she comes running up to me, all pale and trembling and says:

" 'Oh, Jep, do me a favor, will you?'

" 'Why, certainly, Lily,' I says. 'You and the Hernes are my best friends, aren't you?'

" 'I hope you and Meg Herne will always be my friends, Jep,' she says in that quiet voice of hers. 'I'm going to need your help now. I've got another job as cook, in one of the big sanatoriums on the Lake. I just heard today in answer to my application, and I'm leaving tonight while I—' She turns all red in the face with shame, Miss Cherry, not liking me to know her husband treated her so badly. 'While I still have some money,' she sort of gasps. 'It's a live-in job, Jep, and I can't take Rudie with me, but it means I get my room and food free so I can send every cent I earn to Meg. She'll see that my boy has warm clothes and plenty to eat. You tell her to expect a money order once a week, won't you, Jep? And you keep an eye on the boy too, please. I wish —I wish he had a father like you.'"

Jep clenched his powerful hands. "Well, Miss Cherry, it was all I could do to keep from crying like a baby, but I promised her that Meg and I'd take care of Rudie, and I tried to, too, although my own Mouse was taking up most of my free time about then. And Fowler wouldn't let me have anything to do with the boy. I talked to Rudie a couple of times on the street, but he wouldn't listen to me. Kept saying he hated his mother and was glad she'd run away. I couldn't make him believe she'd only gone off to earn money for him, because, you see, the money never came. I don't know what happened to Lily, but Meg never received one cent."

"I know what happened," Cherry said shrewdly. "Mrs. Fowler has been sending money orders with the letters she writes Rudie. But the boy tears them up without even opening the envelopes. And I can guess why. His father probably opened the first one, and, when he found that instead of cash it contained a money order payable to Mrs. Herne, he tore it up in a rage. And after that, Rudie, convinced by his father that his mother had run away so she could spend what she earned on herself, followed his example."

"That's most likely what happened," Jep agreed soberly, "so you can see now, Miss Cherry, what kind of a man Fowler is. You mustn't go there alone tonight. Wait until I can go with you. I'll be back on the day shift in another week."

"Don't be silly, Jep," Cherry said with a smile. "I'm not the least bit afraid, and you can't ever go with me. Fowler or somebody else would recognize you out of uniform, and turn you over to Calahan."

The big doorman frowned. "Calahan was always a friend of mine, Miss Cherry, but I guess you're right. It would be only his duty to turn me in. So you get Jerry Herne to go with you. Fowler's afraid of the Hernes because the owner thinks so highly of Meg, and so he should. A grand woman is Meg Herne, giving Rudie food off her own plate after Lily went away."

The taxi was coming around the bend in the driveway and Cherry felt that under the circumstances she could mumble a little white lie. "I'll get help from the Hernes," she promised Jep as he put her in the cab.

Well, she *was* getting help from the Hernes, wasn't she? Meg would have the key to the basement flat waiting for her. But Cherry had no intention of asking anyone to go with her to No. 29.

"Three would definitely be a crowd," she decided as the taxi carried her down the hill away from Spencer. "Rudie might confide in me, but he wouldn't dare say anything in front of a neighbor that might be carried back to his father."

Ten minutes later the cab stopped in front of No. 27 Duele Street. She paid the driver and hurried inside to ring the Hernes' bell.

She rang and rang but the buzzer did not click in answer. Cherry stood there in the dark, musty-smelling vestibule wondering what could have happened? Where were the Hernes? Even if Meg and Jerry had been called away surely they would have left the key with one of the nine children.

And then the door opened and a huge, broad-shouldered man came into the hallway. For a terrified minute she thought he might be Fowler, but even in the semi-darkness she could see that he had a shock of hair that was redder than Jep's dyed hair. And this big, burly man was grinning cheerfully. Cherry felt sure that Fowler seldom grinned, and when he did, it was not a pleasant sight.

"Miss Cherry Ames?" Jerry Herne asked her. "Meg sent me down with the key. Didn't want you to climb all those stairs."

"Oh, thank you," Cherry said. "Thank you very much, Mr. Herne."

"No trouble at all," he said. "Glad to do anything for a neighbor's child, although if Fowler himself were starving I wouldn't give him a crumb. Well, good luck to you. Just drop the key in our mailbox here when you're through with it."

"Good night," Cherry said. "And thanks again."

In another minute Cherry was in the vestibule next door ringing the superintendent's bell waiting for Rudie to press the buzzer. She waited and waited and at last she came to the disturbing conclusion that Rudie was too sick to crawl out of bed in answer to her ring. What had Miss Gardner said about him to Mrs. Herne that morning? "Rudie was half-asleep." He might have been semiconscious!

Cherry didn't hesitate a minute. She rang all the other bells on the wall at once, and, when the buzzer clacked furiously, she darted inside, calling up the stair well, "Thank you. Visiting nurse calling on the Fowler boy."

Somebody from way up at top shouted back, "Okay, nurse."

She groped her way along the narrow hall that reeked of stale food and was as dusty and badly lighted as Mrs. Herne had described it. Cherry stumbled over an overflowing trash can near the door which she guessed opened on to the cellar stairs. The key fit, but once she was on the other side she was plunged into darkness.

"The fire department ought to hear about this," she muttered, feeling along the wall at the top of the cellar stairs for the light switch. At last she found it, and in the feeble glow from the cobwebby bulb picked her way down the steep, dirty steps.

The air was cold and clammy in the basement and Cherry guessed that the furnace had been allowed to go out. Mildewed and mouse-gnawed cartons of yellowing newspapers were stacked helter-skelter all over the damp floor. Ash cans and trash barrels almost blocked the way to a door that had been left slightly ajar. Cherry determinedly pushed it wide open and stood on the threshold for a minute, staring worriedly inside. It was a big room lighted only by a shadeless, gooseneck student's lamp that stood beside a small cot in one corner. And on the cot, beneath soiled, ragged coverings, lay an emaciated boy who stared at her vacantly.

Cherry controlled an impulse to dash over to him and take him in her arms. But instead she moved slowly across the cluttered room and spoke softly and reassuringly:

"Hello, Rudie. I'm Cherry Ames. Remember me? I came to see how you were getting on." She slipped out of her coat and laid it on the back of the broken chair beside the bed. His eyes were enormous in the thinness of his pale, pinched face, and he continued to stare at her without a spark of recognition. She took off her hat, hoping that without it he might remember the day they had met in the clinic waiting room.

"I've brought you a letter," she said; the word letter might ring a bell. But it didn't, even when she produced the mended pieces of paper he had torn. Cherry leaned closer and it was then that she noticed the fruity odor to his breath.

Acidosis, she thought, shocked by the boy's appearance. And then she remembered his other symptoms: hunger, thirst, loss of weight, a coated tongue, and now the grogginess that meant a near-coma from dehydration and acidosis.

Cherry looked wildly around the room for a telephone. This boy must be brought to the hospital at once for insulin, as well as intravenous fluid. For there was no doubt in Cherry's mind now that Rudie was in an advanced stage of diabetes! There was no phone in the room, and she dashed out and up the stairs, hoping against hope that she might have passed one without seeing it in the hall above. But the walls were blank except for drawings crudely chalked there by the tenement children.

She beat on the door of the first-floor apartment. Nobody home, and there was no time to waste. And then she remembered that around the corner on West Avenue was Palin's drugstore. Surely it would have at least one booth. If not, Mr. Palin would allow her to use his private phone.

Worried as she was about Rudie, Cherry had the presence of mind to prop the front door open with a wedge of newspapers. Then she was flying down the street toward the very place where Jep, that fateful night, had hurried to buy aspirin for his little girl.

And as she ran, Cherry made up her mind. David Lane was the man for this case, for diabetes was his specialty. Alan Dodd, in his slow, cautious way would undoubtedly arrive at the same diagnosis. But David might save precious minutes by giving an immediate injection of insulin.

Then Cherry was in the drugstore phone booth. The nickel wouldn't go into the slot, but at last it did, and she was dialing with icy fingers.

"Children's Hospital, good evening."

"Operator." Cherry forced calmness into her voice. "Operator, this is an emergency, page Dr. David Lane at once."

"Very well, madam." And then: "Sor-ree, Dr. Lane has left the hospital. He signed out a few minutes ago."

Cherry's mind raced. Was David, at this crucial moment, climbing into Leonie Laughton's high-powered car? No, no, she *had* to stop him, for his own sake as well as Rudie's. For Cherry realized now that this was the opportunity she had been waiting for. If David left Leonie to ride in an ambulance to a slum patient, Cherry would have all the evidence she needed to convince Dr. Laughton that David *was* a very serious young man.

"Operator. *Operator!*" But the connection was already broken. Cherry fumbled in her handbag for another nickel. "I've got to catch him before he leaves the Spencer grounds," she mumbled to herself, and dialed the Children's number all over again. "Operator, this is an emergency. Connect me with the doorman at once!"

CHAPTER XII

Danger in the Dark

IT SEEMED LIKE HOURS TO CHERRY BEFORE THE friendly voice of Red Jepson came over the wire:

"Doorman speaking. Good evening."

"Jep!" Cherry knew she was fairly screaming into the mouthpiece, but she couldn't help it. "Jep, this is Cherry Ames."

"Yes, miss," he said disapprovingly. "But please do not call me that. The operator—"

"Red, then," Cherry gasped impatiently. "This is very important. Has Dr. Lane left the building yet?"

"Yes, Miss Cherry. He just now drove off with Miss Laughton."

"Yell after him," Cherry shrieked. "Stop him, Red. You've got to stop him!"

Silence, and then: "I'm sorry, Miss Cherry, but the car is already out of sight."

Cherry let out a long sigh of exasperation. There wasn't time to stop him before he left the Spencer grounds. She'd have to ask Alan to send the ambulance after all. And then she remembered something. "Red, that taxi stand at the bottom of the hill. What's the number? Quick."

He told her and Cherry hung up. Another nickel that wouldn't go into the slot, more frantic dialing, and at last:

"Grogan's taxi, good evening."

"Spencer Hospital," Cherry came back briskly. "This is urgent. One of our doctors is needed at once. He will be passing your stand in another minute in a maroon roadster driven by a girl. I'll hold on while you hail him and call him to the phone."

"A maroon roadster? Yeah, it's coming down the hill now. Okay, ma'am."

Cherry held her breath and then let it out in a rush of words as soon as David said crisply, "Dr. Lane. What is it?"

"Dave," she cried, very near to tears with relief. "This is Cherry Ames. I'm at No. 29 Duele Street. There's a very sick little boy here, and I'm quite sure he has diabetes. Can you come at once in an ambulance?"

"Right," he said promptly. "What apartment and what name?"

"Fowler," she told him, "the super. In the basement. I'll leave both the entrance and the cellar doors ajar so you—"

The operator interrupted: "Five cents for another three minutes, please."

Cherry hung up, there was nothing more to say. It had taken only three minutes and it had seemed like three hours! But the worst was over now. David, she knew, would not waste a second. She could count on the ambulance arriving in another fifteen minutes at the latest.

Cherry unfolded the door to the phone booth and suddenly her knees began to knock together. She couldn't walk back to No. 29—she could hardly walk across the store to the soda fountain. "See here, Ames," she told herself firmly as she sat on the stool and forced her trembling legs to be still, "get a grip on yourself. The whole evening has been pretty exciting, sure, but you're a nurse, not a butterfly. *Stop fluttering!*"

"Feeling dizzy, nurse?"

Cherry looked up into the friendly eyes of the pharmacist. "No, just weak," she said. "I'll be all right in a minute."

"A cup of hot tea," he said firmly. "You girls work too

hard in this district. I'll bet you forgot to eat supper."

Cherry sipped the steaming tea gratefully. She *hadn't* eaten much dinner—she'd been too excited then. Better nibble the tempting crackers he was setting in front of her. David might well want to keep her on the case, and if so, heaven knows when she'd have a chance again to eat. Cherry knew she couldn't do anything for her patient now, but later she might be badly needed.

"Thank you, Mr. Palin," she said when she had finished the last crumb. "What do I owe you?"

"Not a cent," he said, walking with her to the door. "I'd never charge a visiting nurse for a bite to eat at any time. Drop in again, miss."

Now that's a nice man, Cherry thought as she hurried away, feeling full of pep again. I know he hated testifying against Jep during the trial. If only Mr. Palin hadn't been so sure of the time . . .

And then Cherry remembered why she had come to see Rudie Fowler: To disprove Fowler's alibi!

"Oh, dear," she moaned, "even if Rudie responds beautifully to the insulin, it'll be two hours before he'll be fully conscious, and even then Dave probably won't allow me to upset him by asking any questions."

That, she decided, would just have to wait, but the boy would be safe and sound in the hospital where he would be kept for two or three weeks. And Cherry would have plenty of opportunities to visit him on Gwen's ward. Jep, too, would be safe since the chances were that no one else would see through his disguise. But what about Fowler? Suppose he lost his job, as Mrs. Herne had hinted, and moved away to another section of the city. He might even change his name to avoid any responsibility connected with the sick boy, about whom he obviously cared nothing.

Cherry hastened her steps. She would have to pay another visit to No. 29 Duele Street—and soon!

In the vestibule she was chagrined to find that some returning tenant had dislodged her wedge of newspapers, so now she would have to disturb someone in order to get back inside. Absent-mindedly she pressed one bell after another, and at last the top one, before the buzzer clacked. Evidently nobody was home in the building except the top-floor tenants. Thank goodness they weren't out too, Cherry reflected. Otherwise, how could she have returned to her patient?

She pushed the front door open and then stopped as she heard someone coming up the steps behind her. "Good evening," she said, courteously holding the door ajar.

"Good evening yourself," said David Lane. "I telephoned from the taxi stand and got an okay from Al to take the case. He's sending an ambulance and I came on ahead in a cab. You sounded as though the case was pretty urgent." He followed Cherry down the dark hall. "Leonie put up an argument when I asked her to drive me here, so I left her at the bottom of the hill. I doubt if she'll ever speak to me again. My last words to her were 'If I had the time I'd give you a good spanking.'"

Cherry stared at the cellar door. She had left it open purposely. But now it was closed. Had Fowler come back? She shrugged and turned the knob. It didn't matter, now that David was here. Dr. Lane's presence would convince the man that Rudie should be hospitalized.

"Here, let me go first," David interrupted her thoughts. "You'll break your neck on these steep steps."

Halfway down he turned to give Cherry a hand so he did not notice what she *thought* she saw: a shadow moving quickly across the damp cellar wall toward the furnace room. Cherry called out sharply:

"Fowler? *Fowler!* Are you back? It's the nurse and a doctor to see your boy."

No answer.

"Is the boy alone?" David demanded. "Surely his parents—"

"The boy was not only left alone," Cherry broke in,

"but he's been badly neglected. I hope the ambulance gets here soon." And then they heard the high, thin wail of the siren.

As David examined the boy, Cherry gave him a brief history of the case. He didn't waste time asking her why she happened to be here in a visiting nurse's uniform; in fact, Cherry doubted if he had any idea what she had on.

"You were perfectly right, Cherry," he said soberly. "This kid's condition is very serious, but he'll be all right as soon as we put him on insulin."

The bell was ringing furiously and Cherry raced across the room to press the buzzer on the wall. In another minute the ambulance attendants were gently carrying Rudie out on a small stretcher.

"Come along, Cherry," David said, starting after them. "I'd like you to stay on the case, if you will. It'll be a break for Gwen too."

Cherry nodded. "I'll be there when he's brought up from Emergency, don't worry, but first I want to pack a few of his things. It'll make a difference when he's fully conscious if he finds something familiar like his own bathrobe or slippers near by." To herself, she added: *"And* maybe a letter from his mother."

"You're a very thoughtful young lady," Dr. Lane said approvingly. "I'll see you later on Medical."

After he had gone, Cherry turned on all the lights. The room looked as though it hadn't been swept or dusted since Mrs. Fowler's departure. Under the cot, almost hidden by mounds of gray fluff, she found a pair of scuffed, paper-thin slippers. And finally she discovered, hanging on a nail in the back of the cluttered wardrobe, a pathetically worn little robe.

"Never mind," Cherry said, stuffing them into her paper bag, "he's used to them, and that's what counts." Something crackled and Cherry jumped. Was she going to have the good luck of finding one of his mother's letters in the boy's bathrobe pocket? Cherry probed excitedly. It was an envelope all right—and laboriously printed on the upper left-hand corner was Mrs. Lily Fowler's address. Rudie had been too sick to tear this letter up!

Cherry held it against the dusty bulb in the gooseneck lamp. An official-looking slip of paper—a money order—showed clearly through the cheap envelope! Cherry tucked it into her handbag thinking:

"The next time Mrs. Herne visits Medical she'll be bringing two of the kids presents, and I'll bet Rudie's will be a nice warm robe."

Cherry pulled the string on the gooseneck lamp and turned off the other lights she had turned on, pressing a wall button beside the door. Too late she realized that it was too dark for her to pick her way safely through the trash to the stairs. And at the same moment someone grabbed her from behind and dragged her back inside the basement apartment.

Cherry was so surprised she couldn't cry out, not, she realized with a growing sense of terror, that it would have done any good. The crowd of curious onlookers who had probably gathered in front of No. 29 when the ambulance arrived had long ago dispersed. And the tenants on the top floor, could they hear her if she screamed?

She quickly decided against screaming for more reasons than one. The man who was digging his fingers so cruelly into her arms, must be Fowler, and the last thing she wanted to do was to let him know that she was frightened.

For Cherry *was* frightened, so much so that she could only stand there in the darkness, wondering if he had been on the other side of the door, watching her and waiting until the crowd on the street above melted away. Had he seen her search the apartment and tuck the letter in her handbag?

He released her then, slamming the door and turning on the lights almost simultaneously. Cherry whirled around hoping she didn't look as terrified as she felt. Before she could say a word he growled at her menacingly:

"Just who do you think you are, barging in here and sending my boy off in an ambulance?"

"I'm a nurse," Cherry said defiantly, "and Rudie is a very sick little boy."

"Sick! Lazy you mean," he snarled, and added suspiciously, "If you're a nurse why didn't you go along in the ambulance instead of snooping around in my belongings?"

So he *had* been watching her—and waiting! But suddenly Cherry wasn't frightened any more, she was mad, good and mad. "I wasn't snooping," she told him boldly. "I merely stayed behind to pack a few of Rudie's things. If you were any kind of a father you would have been here to do it yourself."

His pale blue eyes narrowed to slits. "It's none of your business what kind of a father I am. What we're talking about is what kind of a nurse you are. I've a good mind to turn you over to the police!"

If he only would, Cherry thought without hope. Where was Calahan now? She pushed back her sleeve to glance at her wrist watch. Nine-thirty. Calahan would be five minutes away on West Avenue, passing the drugstore. Glancing at her own watch gave Cherry an idea. Somehow, this very night, she would find out if Fowler had the missing gold watch!

"My watch has stopped," she lied coolly, "but it must

be getting late. I can't stand here talking with you all night. Do you want to ride back to the hospital with me in a cab?"

He laughed humorlessly. "Don't be in such a hurry, nurse. You're not leaving here for a long, long time. And what makes you think I want to go to that hospital where you sent the kid."

"Oh, but you must, Mr. Fowler," Cherry said, completely in control of the situation now. "Rudie is really dangerously ill. Delirious," she lied shrewdly. "Talking wild, you know. Why, before the doctor came he was trying to tell me something about a radio program and a pawnshop robbery. It didn't make any sense to me, but I'm sure it will to you. Something is worrying him. You'll want to find out what it is and put his mind at rest, I'm sure."

Fowler's ugly face darkened and then he turned white to the lips. "Babbling, is he?" he muttered under his breath. "If that kid squeals I'll—" He stopped himself just in time and forced himself to smile and say in an almost pleasant voice:

"Why, sure, nurse, I'll go along with you. Wouldn't want a sick kid to worry about anything. Guess I've been too busy to notice he wasn't doing so well. It's a lot of work, looking after these three buildings with no help since his mother ran away and left us. It's *her* fault more than mine that the boy's fallen off so much."

He opened the door for her in an obvious effort to make up for his previous ill-treatment of her. At the top of the stairs Cherry handed him the key to the cellar door. "Jerry Herne gave it to me," she explained. "It was Mrs. Herne who notified me that Rudie needed medical attention."

"Why, yes," he said affably. "When Jerry got the key from me he said Meg was going to drop in to see if the boy had eaten the supper I fixed for him. Didn't say anything about a nurse, though." Out in the vestibule he stopped suddenly. "Say," he demanded in a harsh, suspicious voice, "how sick is he, anyway? So sick they maybe won't even let his father see him tonight?"

This was the opening in the conversation Cherry had been praying for. "Oh, I think I can arrange it, Mr. Fowler," she said cheerfully. "That is, if it isn't too late. What time is it, anyway?"

He reached into his pocket and glanced swiftly at his watch, but not so swiftly that Cherry's sharp eyes missed the gleam of gold in that dimly lighted entrance. "If we hurry to the corner" he told her, "and get a cab right away, we'll arrive at the hospital before ten. Will that be too late?" He shifted uneasily into a whine. "I've just got to see my poor little boy tonight, nurse. You'll fix it so I can, won't you?"

Cherry nodded. "I'm sure I can, but let's hurry." To herself she added: "I'll not let him leave Spencer until I've had a look at the back of that watch!"

~~~~~~

CHAPTER XIII

Cherry Sets a Trap

THEY WAITED ON THE CORNER OF DUELE STREET AND West Avenue for several minutes before a cab finally drew up to the curb in answer to Fowler's impatient whistle. Cherry settled back against the cushions and began to plan.

By the time the taxi started up the hill to Spencer, she knew exactly what she was going to do in order to get a look at the back of the gold watch in Fowler's pocket. She could do it with Gwen's help, but if Rudie were brought up to Medical during one of Gwen's rest periods, Cherry would have to divulge her plan to David Lane. That would mean telling him the whole story, but Cherry was so sure the story was going to come to a happy ending that night she didn't worry.

And then she remembered something that upset her

more than any of the night's events. What would Jep Jepson do when he opened the door of the cab and found that she had driven up with Fowler? Would he be so surprised that he couldn't help giving himself—and her—away? And even if he managed to keep his face expressionless, wouldn't Fowler, in the brightly lighted area at the entrance, see through Jep's slim disguise?

No one at Spencer had ever seen the fugitive from justice, but Fowler had known him very well. Mrs. Herne would undoubtedly have recognized her neighbor, no matter what uniform he was wearing, but fortunately, she had never visited the hospital when Jep was on duty.

Cherry tried to unscramble her thoughts. What had Jep said earlier, just before she told him that she knew who he was? Something about "A bite of supper at six, and a sandwich and a cup of coffee *at ten*."

Now Cherry honestly wanted to know the time. She didn't dare risk arousing Fowler's suspicions by asking him to look at his watch again. And yet, having said that her own watch had stopped, she couldn't very well glance at it now. She could, of course, under the pretense of winding it, have a peek, but that didn't fit in with the rest of her scheme.

The watch Charlie had given her when she went in

training would have to stay "stopped" until after she had seen the back of Fowler's. There was nothing to do but sit there in an agony of suspense, praying that someone else was on duty at Children's entrance.

As the cab came around the bend Cherry saw with a sigh of relief that one of the engineers was standing out in front, his only badge of duty, the doorman's blue-and-gold cap.

He came forward to open the door of the cab and stared in surprise when Fowler followed Cherry out. "A patient's father," Cherry explained as she paid the driver. Then she hurriedly led the way up the steps and across the rotunda to the waiting room.

"Make yourself comfortable here, Mr. Fowler," Cherry said. "I'll be back as soon as I can."

She raced out and up the stairs to the second floor. Gwen, her arms full of linen, was bustling into an empty private room. "Am I ever glad to see you," she cried, dumping the towels and sheets into Cherry's arms. "Get this room ready, will you? We've got a kid coming up from Emergency any minute. A diabetic, in very bad shape I understand."

"I know," Cherry said. "Rudie Fowler. Has he had his insulin yet?"

Gwen nodded. "They've done the blood and urine tests and he's due for another intravenous sometime tonight. That is, unless we can get enough fluid into him orally. If you're a friend of mine, you'll sit right here and spoon it into him for the next two hours."

"Of course I will," Cherry said. "You must be dead on your feet."

"I am." Gwen grinned harassedly. "But I go off for an hour at ten-thirty. Thank heavens you turned up when you did." She ran out of the room.

Cherry had barely time to make the bed before an orderly wheeled in Rudie. The boy looked a little brighter, but not nearly so improved as he would in another couple of hours. The orderly, she noticed out of the corner of her eye, stared at her with the same surprised expression the engineer had had on his face when Fowler followed her out of the cab.

She decided she must have a smudge of dust from the basement tenement on her nose, but before she could inspect her face, David Lane came in, very much the young assistant resident now. He smiled at Cherry briefly and said:

"The patient is not dangerously dehydrated and I'd rather not risk upsetting him by ordering another intravenous unless it's absolutely necessary. See how much fluid you can force orally. I'll look in on him again in an hour. He started out of the room and Cherry stopped him hastily with:

"The boy's father, Dr. Lane, is downstairs waiting to see him."

He shrugged. "Well, he'll just have to wait until after I examine the patient again at eleven."

Cherry bit her lip nervously. Would Fowler stay downstairs all that time alone with his guilty thoughts? She was sure he wouldn't. He was already on edge, fearing the boy in his delirium was telling the doctors and nurses what really had happened the night of the pawnshop robbery. Wouldn't he soon suspect that Cherry had lured him to the hospital in order to trap him? Desperate, Cherry dropped her professional manner and said pleadingly:

"David, please stay here while I spoon the first four ounces of fluid into Rudie. I've got something to tell you that's very important. It concerns Dot Jepson as well as Rudie Fowler." As she spoke Cherry was arranging pillows behind Rudie's head, and now she said to him:

"Come on, honey, I'm going to give you some nice cold water, just a drop at a time. It'll make you feel much better. I know how thirsty you are. Remember the day we met? I asked you then if you'd had ham for breakfast. But I was wrong. You hadn't had *any* breakfast, had you?"

A gleam of recognition flickered in and out of Rudie's eyes, but he opened his mouth obediently. As Cherry slowly fed him with a spoon, David Lane straddled a chair at the foot of the bed.

"Give, Cherry," he said. "I'm off duty tonight so I might as well sit here as anywhere else until eleven."

Cherry began at the beginning, interspersing the story with encouraging remarks to her little patient who was as docile as a lamb. He didn't seem to be listening, but when Cherry told David what Rudie had said to Calahan the morning after the crime, the boy suddenly interrupted feebly:

"My pop—he made me—he made me lie to the cop."

"It's all right, honey," Cherry said soothingly, and noticed with satisfaction that the first four ounces were gone. "We understand. And you don't have to be afraid of your father any more. You're going to stay here with us until your mother comes back. She's been saving every penny so she can buy you nice clothes and good things to eat." Cherry snatched Lily Fowler's letter out of her handbag and slit the envelope with one quick flick of her fingernail. "See?" She drew out the money order. "When Mrs. Herne brings this to the post office they'll give her fifty dollars, and it's all for you, Rudie."

He stared at the check doubtfully and then a wan smile spread over his thin face. Cherry held another glass of water to his lips and he drank thirstily and happily, as though he knew now that everything was going to be all right. When he had finished the second four ounces, he sank back on the pillows and closed his eyes.

"We'll let him sleep for awhile," David said quietly. "Finish the story, Cherry."

She told him the rest of it in a whisper, ending with: "Please let Fowler come up now, David, so I can get a look at the back of his watch."

He hesitated. "We-ell, all right. He certainly can't do any harm to you or the kid here." He started for the door. "I'll call the admitting office and have them send Fowler right up."

Cherry waited, hardly daring to think. Suppose Fowler had already bolted?

At last Gwen appeared with the stoop-shouldered man in tow. "I'm going off now, Ames," she said crisply, "leaving a student nurse at the desk. She'll notify you when Mr. Fowler's ten minutes are up."

When she had gone Cherry closed the door and said softly, "Rudie's asleep now, and has been half-asleep ever since he was admitted. He's hardly spoken a word."

Fowler's tense features relaxed, and Cherry went on smoothly:

"I'll leave you alone with him as soon as I've taken his pulse." She put her fingers on the boy's thin wrist and glanced at her own watch. "Oh, dear, what a nuisance. My watch still isn't running. Has yours got a second hand, Mr. Fowler?"

He shook his head up and down, staring at the boy's face, as though he had hardly heard her question.

"Then, please, could I borrow it?" Cherry went on. "I hate to waste any of your precious ten minutes by going out to the desk and borrowing the student nurse's."

Still staring thoughtfully at his son, he reached into his pocket and handed her the big gold watch. "Do you remember exactly what the kid said to you, nurse?" he asked.

"Why, no," Cherry said, turning slightly so that she could look at the back of the watch without his seeing her. "Something about the radio and a robbery. I guess he was trying to tell me what an exciting program he had been listening to before I came to see him."

There could be no doubt about it—the initials were H. T. A.!

Holding the watch, face uppermost, in the palm of one hand, Cherry kept her fingers on Rudie's pulse for another minute. She was about to return the watch to Fowler when he suddenly snarled:

"Hey, give me that!" He roughly snatched it away from her and thrust it in his pocket. "Say, what kind of a nurse are you? Don't you know enough to keep your own watch running?"

Cherry's heart sank and she realized that when she turned away from the bed to look at the monogram Fowler could have seen her reflection in the mirror over the dresser. Now, there was no time to be lost. She controlled her growing excitement with an effort and said blandly:

"It *was* stupid of me to let my watch run down. And thank you very much for letting me borrow yours, Mr. Fowler." She forced herself to smile at him. "I'll run along now and leave you alone with your son. If he wakes up, try to get him to drink a little water, won't you?"

His pale brows were drawn together in an ugly scowl. "That's your job, not mine. What do I pay taxes for, anyway?"

Cherry didn't bother to answer as she slipped out and closed the door behind her. *If only she could lock it!*

The long corridor leading from the private pavilion to the ward was deserted, and eerily quiet, as though nobody on the whole floor had any intention of helping Cherry catch a thief. Where was the probie David had promised to send her in case she had to leave her patient? Where was David himself? Probably down in

Emergency checking on all the various tests and X rays they had given Rudie. Why, oh, why, hadn't she asked him to stay on Medical until after she had seen Fowler?

Who *was* on Medical besides the uninterested specials behind the closed doors she was flying past? Probably nobody but a few student nurses. If only Gwen were sitting at her desk instead of napping peacefully over at Crowley!

Cherry dashed by the private rooms and skidded to a stop at the desk. A pretty student nurse was sitting there and she looked up at Cherry quizzically.

"Oh, you must be Mrs. Fowler," she said sweetly, glancing at the chart in her hand. "Now, you mustn't worry about your little boy. He's going to be perfectly all right. You're very fortunate that one of our nurses stopped Dr. Lane just as he was going off duty. He has a marvelous record with diabetics."

Cherry gaped. Then slowly it dawned on her that she was still in her visiting nurse uniform which, to a student nurse, would look like any other trim blue suit. She had left her hat back at No. 29 and her white blouse was as wilted as a piece of string.

No wonder the temporary doorman and the orderly who had brought Rudie from Emergency had stared at her! Gwen, who had warned her against this very event, had been too harassed and tired to notice. And

David Lane, at first completely absorbed in his patient and then, by Cherry's story, had obviously no idea that she was wearing blue instead of head-to-toe white.

Cherry set her jaw. It was too late to worry about her violation of rules and regulations now. The important thing was to get this student nurse into action by convincing her that she was Cherry Ames, an R.N.

She smiled sweetly back at the pretty girl, stifling her impatience. "Listen, honey, do I look old enough to be the mother of an eleven-year-old boy?"

The student nurse glanced again at the chart and then flushed. "Oh, no, of course not. Then who are you?"

"Pay no attention to my outfit," Cherry said briskly, "but believe it or not, I'm an R.N. The one who called Dr. Lane back on duty."

The girl jumped to her feet. "Oh, my goodness, then you must be Cherry Ames. Miss Jones told me you were temporarily specialing the Fowler boy until he's well enough to be brought in here. Oh, dear, Miss Ames—I had no idea—"

Cherry waved away her apologies. "Pick up that phone," she said crisply, "and have Dr. Lane paged. It is vital that he comes to the Fowler boy's room at once."

The embarrassed student nurse was chattering into the mouthpiece as Cherry hurried back to the private pavilion. Somehow she would have to keep Fowler there until David arrived.

Just before she reached Rudie's temporary quarters, a door opened and out marched a tall, gray-headed nurse in a uniform so stiffly starched that Cherry thought she could hear it crackle as the Night Supervisor came swiftly down the corridor toward the ward!

CHAPTER XIV

The Trap Is Sprung

CHERRY STOOD STOCK-STILL AS MRS. WELCH, THE NIGHT Supervisor, marched briskly nearer and nearer. If only there were an empty private room Cherry could dodge into! But she knew that Rudie Fowler was temporarily occupying the only vacant room on the floor.

Cherry's knees turned to water. Oh, if it only were true what Dr. Laughton had said about an Indian in full regalia receiving merely a passing glance! He obviously hadn't included the Night Supervisor in that blanket statement, for Cherry knew from her special duty experience that Gwen had been right when she had said that the formidable Mrs. Welch was "a stiff-necked martinet who's everywhere at once and never misses a trick." Gwen had summed up the Night Supervisor with:

"Woe betide the nurse who meets with her disapproval!"

For a fleeting second Cherry prayed hopelessly for a fairy godmother, who, with a tap of her wand, could transform her from a visiting nurse without an assignment to a comparatively inconspicuous Indian chief in full war paint.

"My cheeks are probably red enough as they are," she thought with grim humor. "But, oh, for a tomahawk so I could chop a hole in the floor and sink down through it!"

Cherry felt like a drowning person going down for the third time as scene after scene flashed across her imagination, keeping time to the steady beat of the Supervisor's approaching footsteps. "A dismissal . . . the disgrace, never to be lived down . . . the puzzled frown on her mother's sweet face . . . her father trying to disguise his disappointment behind his warm smile . . . and Dr. Joe, who had inspired her to take up nursing . . . Dr. Joe who had warned her:

"No pranks, Cherry."

Cherry suddenly squared her shoulders. This *wasn't* a prank. The result of her scheme would bring about the health and happiness of two Children's patients. A dismissal was unimportant in a case like this.

*Fowler must be caught with the watch in his posses-
sion this very night!*

And then Cherry saw him slink out of Rudie's room,
and, at the same moment, the Night Supervisor came
to an abrupt halt, halfway between Cherry and Fowler.

"Miss Ames." Her voice rang out in the silent corridor. "What does this mean? Do my eyes deceive me?
Are you working on this floor improperly uniformed?"

The question, delivered practically in the roar of a
drill sergeant on the parade ground, made, Cherry saw
to her consternation, even Fowler jump. He glanced
swiftly in her direction, and then scurried away toward
the east end of the corridor. It gave Cherry some small
comfort to realize that this gave her a few minutes'
grace, since the east elevators did not run after nine
o'clock.

While she was keeping an eye on Fowler, Cherry
answered the Night Supervisor:

"I'm sorry Mrs. Welch, I *am* improperly uniformed.
I was called out on emergency duty and didn't have
time to change."

Mrs. Welch beetled her pepper-and-salt eyebrows.
"What exactly do you mean, Miss Ames, by the word
change? If you were in street clothes I might let you
off with a reprimand. But you happen to be wearing the

uniform of a visiting nurse. I shall give you three seconds to explain why."

Three seconds! Cherry thought desperately. Even if she was a proficient liar, she couldn't invent a convincing excuse in three years! It would take forever to make this martinet understand why she had *had* to wear her visiting nurse's uniform that evening.

And Cherry did not have forever, for Fowler was coming back now, moving slowly and unobtrusively, keeping close to the wall, but in another few minutes he would reach the west elevators, which *were* running.

Cherry took a deep breath. "I simply can't explain now, Mrs. Welch," she began meekly. "I—I—my patient needs me."

Mrs. Welch drew herself up to her full height, of almost six feet, Cherry thought. "Your patient does not need you immediately," she said sternly. "I just looked in on him and he was sleeping soundly with his father sitting beside him."

"That's just the point," Cherry blurted. "His father *isn't* with him any more. That's Mr. Fowler sneaking along the corridor, Mrs. Welch, and he's—he's—"

Oh, what was the use? It was too long a story, and one which, even if told unhurriedly, would sound completely fabricated to the outraged Night Supervisor.

Mrs. Welch whirled around and immediately Fowler

began to walk more boldly. Even Cherry had to admit that he looked like any other father leaving the floor after a visit with his sleeping son. The Supervisor wheeled to face Cherry again. She said evenly:

"I have no idea what you have been up to this evening, Miss Ames, but perhaps you are right. You had better return to your patient. It will no doubt be the last patient you ever have here, for I shall of course report you to the administrator and recommend that you be dismissed."

Cherry gulped. Fowler was passing them now, moving swiftly toward the elevators. "I can't return to my patient," she thought wildly, very near to tears. "I've got to run after him and keep the elevator man from carrying him down to the ground floor."

"Oh, Mrs. Welch," she begged, starting after the Supervisor, "please don't make me—"

"Make you what, Cherry Ames?" a soft voice at her elbow asked.

Cherry stopped, clenching her small fists. This was the end. To have Dr. Van Laughton of all people show up now! He wouldn't hesitate to order her out of the hospital then and there.

"Oh, Dr. Laughton," Mrs. Welch was saying, "I'm so glad you turned up. I shall leave Miss Ames to you. No explanation is necessary, I feel sure, when I tell you that I recommend her dismissal from Spencer Hospital."

She was gone, her starched skirts crackling. And Fowler now had his thumb on the elevator button! It was all Cherry could do to keep from screaming as the Chief said, pointing a small finger at her accusingly:

"What are you doing on this floor in that uniform, Cherry Ames?"

Cherry swallowed the scream in her throat and tried to answer, but no words came. She was hypnotized by the sight of Fowler and the glowing light above his head which showed that the elevator was coming up. It wasn't until the doors actually opened that Cherry found her voice:

"Stop that man, Dr. Laughton," she gasped. "We've got to stop him. He's a thief, and he's got a stolen watch in his pocket right now."

The doors clanged shut as Fowler slipped inside, but Dr. Laughton had Cherry by the hand and was flying toward the nearest telephone. Cherry knew how Alice must have felt when the Red Queen dragged her along, shouting, "Faster, faster," in *Through the Looking Glass*.

Dr. Laughton wasn't shouting anything, but his feet seemed to skim above the floor until he finally stopped by a wall recess and disappeared inside. Cherry heard him say crisply into the telephone:

"Dr. Laughton speaking. Admitting desk." And then: "Dr. Laughton speaking. A man is just stepping out of the west visitors' elevator. Stop him, and keep him there on any excuse you can invent until I get down."

He popped out of the telephone recess so quickly that Cherry jumped. "Hurry, girl," he said crisply. "Give me the facts. We can't hold that man downstairs all night."

Cherry saw with relief that a probie was hurrying into Rudie's room, and guessed that Mrs. Welch had sent her to take Cherry's place until she was released— or fired, by Dr. Laughton. It was now Cherry's turn to grab the doctor by the hand.

"Come on," she said. "Let's not wait for an elevator. Let's walk. I'll tell you what happened on the way."

Quickly she gave him the high lights of the night's events, and on the landing he stopped with a chuckle.

"I heard about Davie's visit to the slums from my very angry little granddaughter. She's of the opinion now that he's too much of a boor to make a good resident. She aroused my curiosity about that emergency case which made Davie leave her at the bottom of the hill, so I thought I'd drop in and see what it was all about."

"Well, now you know everything," Cherry said impatiently. "Can't you telephone for the police right away?"

"I certainly can," he said, turning around. "And the nearest phone is at the top of the stairs. You go on ahead down and keep Fowler on the premises somehow. You can do it easily, Cherry Ames. Smartest nurse I ever ran across in my whole career."

Cherry made the turn on the landing and darted down the last flight of steps. At the bottom she saw to her horror that Fowler was paying no attention to the nurse who was beckoning to him from the admitting desk. He was hurrying across the rotunda, and when he saw her, he broke into a run. Not an intern, an elevator man, or an orderly was in sight. If only David or Alan would suddenly appear on the scene!

But they didn't, and Fowler had almost reached the door when it suddenly opened from the outside. And then Cherry did scream, at the top of her lungs:

"Jep, *Jep!* Stop him. It's the thief, Fowler, and he's got the watch in his pocket right now."

Fowler, startled by Cherry's loud accusation, lost his balance, and stumbled right into the doorman's strong arms.

During the ensuing tussle, the rotunda, which had been so maddeningly deserted only a minute before, became as populated as a busy railroad terminal. White-coated men, among them both Alan and David, rushed from every direction to help Jep keep the writhing, thrashing man a prisoner.

But Jep needed no help. With one hand he kept Fowler's arms pinned behind him. By the time Cherry got there, Jep had already extricated the watch. He handed it to her with a grave smile: "This what you wanted, Miss Cherry?"

Cherry felt like laughing and crying at once as she passed the watch along to David for safekeeping. Fowler heaved his heavy shoulders, struggling to wrench himself free, and thrust his face close to Cherry's, snarling:

"You tricked me, you—you, detective! I should have known you weren't a nurse. Poking around in my belongings without a warrant, and pretending your watch was broken."

David pulled her protectively away from the man's ugly face, but Cherry laughed. "You're quite right, Fowler, about one thing. My watch does keep perfect time. But I *am* a nurse, not a detective."

"I'm not so sure of that," a low voice said, and Cherry looked around to find Dr. Laughton standing there.

His face was expressionless, but Cherry's heart sank.

What had he meant by "I'm not so sure of that?" Was he going to punish her after all? A moment ago she had thought he might forgive her for being improperly uniformed. Had Fowler's accusation, "without a warrant," made the Chief change his mind?

"Oh, dear," Cherry moaned inwardly. "I'll never get out of this scrape. Never, never, NEVER!"

CHAPTER XV

"The Wearing of the Blue"

CHERRY, FEELING ALMOST AS GUILTY AS THE CAPTURED criminal himself, listened halfheartedly as Fowler unwittingly screamed out a confession.

"It was that boy of mine who put you on to it," he yelled at Cherry. "I'll fix him for squealing, don't you worry!"

And then they all heard the wail of a siren as the police car climbed the hill to Spencer. Fowler seemed to crumple at the very sound of it, realizing too late that he had given himself away in front of a dozen witnesses.

From then on until midnight Cherry had no time to think about her own worries. First she and Dr. Laughton talked to the sergeant, then after he had questioned David Lane, Cherry was called back to the Chief's office to tell her story all over again from beginning to end. But at last they were all gone, taking both Fowler and Jep with them. Cherry sank exhaustedly into a chair beside Dr. Laughton's desk and said:

"What will they do to Jep, sir? Will he be punished for breaking out of jail?"

"Don't worry about him, girl," the Chief told her. "I've already called my lawyer and ordered him to represent Jep. He's down at the station now. Robson's a smart man. He'll have Jep free and clear in no time flat."

"That's wonderful," Cherry said. "When Dot's discharged she can go home to her father. Jep has a nice job waiting for him."

"So?" The Chief looked disappointed. "I hoped to keep him on here as doorman. Don't tell me you've outwitted me in that, Cherry Ames."

Cherry explained, and Dr. Laughton shook his head. "No, that will never do. Can't have my little adopted granddaughter living in that basement. I've a small cottage on my own place that will suit them both fine." He frowned. "And don't you dare interfere with my plans, girl! You've done enough interfering for one night."

Cherry's cheeks flamed. "I don't know what you mean, sir. If you're referring to my posing as a relief visiting nurse, I can explain."

"We'll take that matter up later," he said. "I'm referring to your running my hospital. The very idea of a chit like you calling a doctor back on duty without authorization!" His eyes twinkled, and Cherry knew that he was only teasing her. "A smart move that," he said approvingly. "Showed me you were right about Davie in more ways than one. Had a chance to talk to him tonight while we were waiting to be questioned by the police sergeant." He rubbed his chin thoughtfully. "Yes, girl, he's the man for the job all right. Anything else on your mind?"

"Yes, sir," Cherry said quickly. "I'm going home for the weekend tomorrow morning, so if you don't mind, I'd like to tell you now more of the background of our two young patients, Dot and Rudie. I had only time earlier to give you the high lights."

Dr. Laughton nodded and took careful notes as Cherry talked.

When she had finished she stood up and said, "Well, I guess that's all. And now I'd better get back to my patient." Then she remembered, and she sank back in her chair. "That is, sir, if I still have a patient."

"Well, yes and no," he said thoughtfully. "I have plans for you, Cherry. I think you've got executive ability that's being wasted in our clinic. I've got a night supervisor job in mind for you. At another hospital. Would you be interested?"

Cherry couldn't believe her ears. Her dream was not only going to come true, but the Chief obviously wasn't angry with her for her violation of rules and regulations. "Would I be interested?" she finally got out. "Oh, Dr. Laughton, I'd hate to leave Children's, but—"

"We'll all hate to lose you," he interrupted, "but we mustn't let our sentiments stand in the way of your progress, my dear. You have a brilliant future in nursing, Cherry Ames. Mark my words, you'll go far." He stood up to shake hands with her across the desk. "Now, is there anything else on that busy mind of yours?"

"Well," Cherry said tentatively. "Mrs. Welch. I— She—I mean, after all . . ."

He threw back his head and roared with laughter. "I had a little chat with Mrs. Welch too while I was waiting for the sergeant to say I could go on about my business. She sees eye to eye with me on several things now, among them your, shall we say 'the wearing of the blue'? I told her you were acting under a blanket order from me to go visiting."

Cherry laughed. "You scared me to death, Dr. Laughton, when you said a while ago that you weren't sure I *was* a nurse."

"I didn't say anything of the kind," he retorted. "I simple said I wasn't sure you *weren't* a detective." He chuckled. "The qualifications that make a good detective also make a good night supervisor, my dear. At your new post you'll have to see everything that goes on, and keep one jump ahead of everybody. You've been several jumps ahead of all of us here ever since you arrived. That's why I'm going to recommend you for the job."

Cherry was so embarrassed and excited she could only mumble "Thanks," and hurry away. Upstairs on Medical, Mrs. Welch was the first one to congratulate her.

"I'm sorry I was so abrupt, Miss Ames," she said apologetically. "I had no idea you were tracking down a criminal in our midst. Good luck to you in your new job. If you like it as much as I do mine, you'll be very happy." She bustled down the corridor.

Gwen looked up from her desk as Cherry approached it. "Will you kindly get off my floor in that outfit?" she said tartly. "Haven't you caused enough excitement around here for one night?" She grinned. "No kidding though, Cherry, you're a heroine. And as such I order you to go over to Crowley and go to bed."

"But don't you need me?" Cherry demanded. "What about the Fowler boy?"

For answer Gwen pointed to a glass cubicle not far

from Dot's. "He's had his fluid and is resting quietly. Don't you think anybody can do anything with children except you, Cherry Ames?"

Cherry giggled. "Nobody ever tells me anything," she moaned.

"Nobody has to it seems," Gwen came back. "Now scram and get some beauty sleep. David Lane won't be happy if you're too tired to dance with him at the party tomorrow night." She looked up at the clock. "Ho-hum, I mean tonight."

Cherry snatched her handbag off the desk and disappeared into a phone booth.

Back at Crowley, Josie was waiting for her. "Good news travels fast, but bad news much faster," she said. "I've never been through such a night. Two hours ago we heard that you had been fired, and just now we heard you're teacher's pet. What *has* been going on over there, Cherry?"

"Not now," Cherry said sleepily. "I'll tell you all about it tomorrow, Josie."

Josie reluctantly scrambled off the bed. "Some girls have all the luck," she said, giving Cherry an affectionate hug, "and get all the men too. Is there any truth in the rumor that somehow during the excitement this evening you and David Lane managed to get yourselves engaged?"

Cherry hugged her back. "No more truth than there was in the rumor that he was engaged to Leonie Laughton," she said. "Dave is simply one of those unfortunately good-looking young men whom gossips will always tie up in a romance."

"I'll take your word for it," Josie said dubiously. "But maybe you'll sing another song after this weekend."

"Maybe I will," Cherry said with a laugh. "And then again, maybe I won't."

CHAPTER XVI

Halloween

ALL FIVE OF THEM SPENT THE FIRST FEW HOURS OF their weekend off duty catching up on their sleep. So it was almost dark when Alan Dodd parked his battered sedan in front of Cherry's home. A crisp breeze was swirling the red and gold leaves across the lawn, and a huge jack-o'-lantern leered at them from one of the windows.

"Charlie's idea of a welcome," Cherry said, tumbling out of the car with the others.

David Lane stretched his long legs. "Is your twin a sleuth too, Cherry? If he is, I can tell you right now I'm not going to play that 'murder' game you were telling us about. Not unless you're both on my side."

"We'll have to play it for Midge's sake," Cherry told him. "It's a Halloween ritual with her. And no,

Charlie, who by the way is as blond as I am dark, has no time to waste on mysteries. He's very serious about his career, and is studying aerial engineering at State College."

"Who said you weren't serious about your career?" David demanded. "You stiff-necked night supervisor, you!"

"Wha-at?" Gwen demanded. "What's this about a night supervisor? Are you holding out on us, Ames?"

Cherry had no time to reply, for at that moment the wind blew the scudding clouds away from the face of the orange harvest moon. And there, looming horridly up from behind a clump of her mother's favorite dahlias, was a frightening apparition. It was at least six feet tall, with a nightmarish face, and it flapped its white shrouds, moaning dismally:

"OH-H-H-H—OH!"

Cherry gasped and then giggled. "Charlie! Get out of those garments and come greet your guests."

As though he had been waiting for this order, Cherry's tall, athletic twin suddenly appeared on the porch. He looked very handsome in his neat, dark-blue, double-breasted suit. "Anything for you, Sis," he said with a grin. "But what's wrong with these garments anyway?"

Cherry raced to meet him halfway up the steps. As they hugged each other, she introduced him to the two young doctors amid the loud groans of the apparition. Charlie unconcernedly shook hands all around.

"Oh, that?" he said in answer to Cherry's pointing finger. "A little something we acquired recently. And I'm afraid it's here to stay. At least for the weekend." He shrugged. "You'll get used to it in time. Sort of grows on you, you know."

The thing was coming toward them now, swaying and tottering through the flower beds. Josie emitted a sound that was half-scream, half-giggle. "Stop it, Charlie," she begged, clutching his arm. "If it comes one step nearer I'll faint."

"Stop, Frankenstein," Charlie said dramatically.

But the thing only moved faster—and then, suddenly it swayed for the last time, and collapsed. "Help," it yelled. "I'm all tangled up in these sheets and stilts."

"Midge!" Cherry flew to the rescue. They all helped to extricate the madcap, laughing teen-ager, who from her undignified position on the ground stared soulfully up at David:

"Oh," she moaned, "you must be Dr. Lane. I'm hurt badly. Take my pulse, feel my fevered brow. Do you think I'll live, doctor?"

David grinned and helped her to her feet. "I'm afraid so. But if not, you'll make a nice corpse for our murder game tonight."

Midge preened, taking this for a compliment. Then

she noticed that Alan Dodd was almost as good looking as David Lane. She extended her small hand with a very queenly elevation of her pretty head. "Welcome, Dr. Dodd," she said, her thick light-brown hair cascading over her shoulders. "It is indeed a pleasure to meet the new Head Resident of the Children's General Hospital."

Alan took her hand soberly. "Thank you, madam, but I'm afraid you have me and my colleague confused."

Midge flamed with embarrassment and immediately became a shamefaced little girl. "Oh, golly," she mumbled to Cherry. "Have I put my foot in it? Will everybody hate me from now on?"

Cherry touched her lips to Midge's wide, shapely mouth, whispering, "Of course not, darling. But don't you think you should greet my feminine guests now?"

Midge, very red in the face now, hastened to hug both Gwen and Josie.

" 'Twas ever thus," Gwen said with a laugh. "Men first, and women and children afterward, eh, Midge?"

Alan, obviously feeling sorry for the humiliated young girl, tucked her hand through his arm. "Pay no attention to those cats," he told her. "They're just jealous because you're going to be my date tonight."

Midge immediately recovered her normal gaiety. "It's Cherry's fault I got you and David mixed up," she told him in an intimate aside. "When she telephoned saying you'd be late she tried to tell me everything that happened last night in three minutes."

"You mean," Cherry corrected her with an affectionate pat, "I tried to answer all of your questions which was pretty difficult considering you never stopped asking 'em once during the whole one-sided conversation."

Midge tossed her head. "I just wanted to prepare you, Cherry," she said loftily. "I've plans—very important ones. After supper and after dancing and after we play murder, we're all going to sit in front of the fire and, instead of telling ghost stories, you're going to tell us how you solved that pawnshop mystery. From beginning to end. Honestly," she told Alan, "the tantalizing letters that girl has been writing home! The suspense has been simply ghastly!"

"I agree with you, Midge," Josie said heartily. "I don't know anything more about what happened last night than you do. Miss Ames refused to talk while we were driving; in fact, if the unglamorous truth be known, she dozed from door to door."

Gwen chuckled. "So did we all. Except poor Alan, the driver. But he's used to going without sleep, having been on night duty for the past two weeks."

Cherry started across the lawn. "You young people can stand out here all night if you like, but I'm going in to greet Mother and Dad. Furthermore, I'm starving!"

She flew up the steps and into the house and then

stood for a minute in the hall, sniffing. The pungent odor of spiced pumpkin pie blended deliciously with the fragrance of roasting, stuffed turkey.

"Mother," Cherry called out. "Dad! Where are you?"

Arm in arm, they appeared at the living-room door then, and in another minute Cherry was kissing them both.

"Glad to be home, nurse?" her father asked, his eyes twinkling.

For answer, Cherry stood on tiptoe to lay her cold cheek against his. "I guess I'm homesick most all the time," she told them, "but I'm generally too busy to give way to it."

And then Dr. Joe Fortune was there too, congratulating Cherry:

"Van Laughton telephoned me this morning about you," he said, smiling at her proudly. "But I haven't said a word to your parents. Thought you'd like to surprise them."

"What's all this mystery?" Mrs. Ames demanded. But there was no time for an answer for the house was soon overflowing with Cherry's gay young guests.

After they had been greeted by her parents, Cherry escorted Gwen and Josie up to her room, while Charlie led the doctors off to his. Cherry's red-and-white dressing table was flanked by a cot, and another one had been set up beside her bed.

"We'll be a little crowded, girls," she said, handing them towels and washcloths," but it'll be more fun this way. The guest room's tiny, so Charlie is bunking in there."

After a delicious supper, Alan Dodd declared that he was too stuffed and sleepy to be anything but the corpse in the murder game. So Cherry, David, and Josie, as private detectives, teamed up against Gwen, Charlie, and Midge, "the police." Cherry's side won, quickly deducing from the clues the *who, when,* and *why* of the case. The *who* turned out to be Dr. Joe Fortune and his motive was that Alan had finished the pumpkin pie before he could ask for a third helping.

At last they were all grouped around the fire in the mahogany-and-blue living room, tired and flushed from an hour of dancing to gay tunes.

"Begin at the beginning, Cherry," Midge ordered, shaking the corn popper.

"Oh, no, please," Mrs. Ames begged, filling tall glasses with homemade cider. "Begin at the happy ending, Cherry. Why did Dr. Joe congratulate you before dinner?"

Cherry explained. "I'm not absolutely sure yet that I'll get the night supervisor job," she said. "I'll have to be interviewed by the administrator and the trustees, of course. And to tell you the truth, I don't even know what hospital Dr. Laughton was talking about. He said he wouldn't tell me until after they had considered his recommendation."

Josie squeezed her hand. "You'll get it," she said fondly. "And you deserve it, too. But now, for heaven's sake, tell us what went on at Children's last night."

Cherry told them then, beginning with her first suspicions that Jep Jepson might be working somewhere at Spencer and ending with:

"And then, to cap the climax, after all I'd been through, I was ordered off the floor by our head nurse here, Miss Gwenthyan Jones."

Gwen chuckled. "And rightly so, but even then you didn't obey me immediately. Whom did you telephone to at that hour of night, Cherry?"

"To Mrs. Lily Fowler," Cherry said, smiling at Midge, who, she knew, had been dying to ask a question for some time. "Acting on the Chief's orders, I told her the whole story. We both felt that Rudie would recuperate more quickly if he were reconciled to his mother as soon as possible."

"Well, go on, don't stop there," Midge shouted impatiently. "Is she coming right away?"

"Better than that," Cherry told her. "She should be there by now, and she's there to stay. Dr. Laughton offered her a nice job in the diet kitchen. Now that

Rudie can see her every day I'm sure he'll get well very fast."

"And," Midge added as triumphantly as though it had been she who had solved everyone's problems, "when Mrs. Fowler turns in all those money-order receipts she'll collect a lot of money from the post office."

"That's right," Cherry said, "and do you know what she's going to do with the money order that wasn't torn up? The one I found in Rudie's bathrobe pocket?"

"I'll bet she gives it to Mrs. Herne," Midge answered, "so that her family can have an enormous turkey and presents and everything on Thanksgiving."

Cherry nodded. "And knowing Meg Herne, I feel sure Dot and Jep will be invited to the party."

Gwen sighed. "One thing you can be absolutely sure of, Ames, is that I'll never doubt your word again. I cringe every time I think of how I laughed when you told me there was an escaped convict in our midst."

"Speaking of your famous floor," Cherry interrupted. "Who was the little probie who got all the fluid into Rudie without my expert help?"

"Polly," Gwen told her smugly. "And it was her first crack at night duty too. She's going to be all right, that one, in spite of what our new Resident may think."

"Who, me?" David demanded. "I always thought Polly would make a swell nurse if she ever got over being afraid of her own shadow. That's why I recommended her for night duty. Figured that as shorthanded as we are, she'd have to show some initiative then."

"You're smart," Gwen said admiringly. "You'll end up as Administrator before you're through."

"No, I won't," David said soberly. "I've at last made up my mind where I want to end up."

"I can guess," Cherry said. "In your dad's shoes."

He nodded, smiling. "I'm nowhere near good enough yet, but someday, Cherry Ames, I'll be a country doctor worth the name. Wait and see."

Cherry smiled back. "I don't expect to wait until I'm old and gray, Dave. You're getting the best experience in the world at Children's. For, after all, as Gwen so aptly put it, when you get right down to it, all sick people are children!"

More thrilling adventures await Cherry in her new job in a country hospital. Don't miss **CHERRY AMES, NIGHT SUPERVISOR** —the exciting story of how Cherry outwits a shrewd criminal and solves the hospital's financial problem.